The Climb

Written by Kendra Nicholson

The Climb

By Kendra Nicholson

© 2020

TheClimb@WriterKendraNicholson.com

1

My school counselor, Mr. Blackwell, came to see me at home last week, and he said he thought it would be a good idea for me to start a journal. I told him it seemed weird to me to write stuff down like a diary, so he said I don't have to do it like that. I could just record myself talking. Just talk like I'm telling stuff to someone I don't know, and it would be a good way to get my feelings out without having to worry about anyone judging me. It actually makes sense, I guess. I'll give it a shot, and if it doesn't feel right, I'll just stop.

It already feels weird. I guess I'll try it again tomorrow.

2

Okay, I'm back. It still feels kind of weird, but I told him I would try it for at least three or four days. So… I don't really know where to start. I think I'll do it like I have an imaginary friend like some little kids do. I don't exactly know what that was like, because I didn't have an imaginary friend. I didn't really need one, because I had my brother.

I don't know what else to say today. Maybe I'll have more tomorrow, because it's my first day back to school. I already dread it.

3

The front doors of the school looked more terrifying than a haunted house. I just stood there for what felt like forever, trying to work up the courage to walk inside. My backpack weighed a ton, because it was full of all my text books and makeup work from being out of class for over two weeks. The thought of taking those last steps and pulling open the doors made my stomach feel weird, like when I have to get up in front of the class to give a presentation.

The five-minute warning bell rang, and startled me out of my daze.

"Well, this is it – it will only be worse if I'm tardy," I mumbled to myself.

"What?" another student stopped to ask. He looked like an eighth grader.

"What?" I said, in a moment of brilliance.

"You said something. I heard you as I was walking by."

"Oh… ummm… no… I didn't. I mean, I did… but I was just… ummm."

"Whatever, dude," he said, and shook his head as he kept going.

Awesome, right? I had already made a fool of myself, and I hadn't even entered the building. I closed my eyes, took a deep breath, hitched up my backpack, and started up the stairs, and through the doors. It wasn't so bad in the hallway, where I was pretty much lost in the shuffle. It probably helped that I'm small for a seventh grader, and most people just looked right over me, but by the time I reached my homeroom door, my heart was pounding and my hands were all sweaty. I wiped them on my jeans, took another deep, shaky breath, and opened the door.

It was even worse than I thought it would be. One by one, the whole class was turning to look at me, and as they did, it got quieter and quieter. It sounded like someone was turning down the volume on the TV, until they all stared at me in total silence. Even Mrs. McKay heard the change in volume, and turned from writing on the whiteboard to see what was happening.

She looked surprised, just for a second, then she tried to smile and said, "Oh! Cody! Welcome back! We missed you."

When I didn't smile back, her smile slowly fell from her face, and she gave me "The Look." It was the same look I got from everybody now. They sort of tilt their head down, and to the side a little bit, then they scrunch up their forehead, and frown. It's the look that people give because they feel sorry for me. Because they don't know what to say.

It was too much. All those eyes, staring at me in silence. I felt my face start to get hot, and my eyes started stinging.

No… no no no no no NOOOOO! I couldn't cry in front of the whole class. *I could not.* But the more I fought it, the more the tears started to build up. I could feel them getting ready to start rolling down my face, and my lip started trembling and…
I panicked.

I dropped my backpack to the floor with a loud smack that made everyone jump, threw open the classroom door, and bolted. I ran down the hall and through the front doors. I heard Mrs. McKay yelling my name, but I didn't stop. I was just running. I needed to get away from the stares, from the sad, sorry looks – from the awkward silence that seemed to follow me everywhere now.

Finally, I ran out of breath and adrenaline, and I had a wicked side cramp. I was doubled over with my hands on my knees, wheezing and shaking all over, my legs all wobbly. When I finally calmed a bit, pulled myself together, and was breathing a little more normally, I realized where I was. I sat down hard and looked up at the old warehouse. I had run to the place where my big brother, Trevor, climbed to the roof and jumped off.

4

Mom was crying. Again. This time it was my fault.

"I'm really sorry, Mom," I said.

"No, Cody, sweetie. It's okay. It's not your fault. I should have known it was too early to let you go back to school."

"Maybe, but I know I scared you, and I didn't mean to. Everyone was just… weird. I freaked out, and – I don't know."

"Cody… why did you go… where you went?"

"I don't know, Mom. I guess I just… wanted to…"

Mom shook her head and said, "Nevermind. We don't have to talk about this right now. Do you want a snack?"

"No. I'm not hungry. I'm going to go to my room now, okay?"

"Of course. Please go. If you need anything, just let me know. And son?"

"Yeah?"

"I love you."

"Yeah, I know, Mom. I love you too."

She was so careful with me now. If I had hauled ass out of the school like that even a month ago, I would have been grounded till I was 30. Then Dad would have come home and bumped it up to 40. Not now though. Now they were treating me like I might go crazy at any moment. After today I wondered if I might, too.

It's pretty scary, to be honest. What if I did? Trevor was just a normal guy until he moved away to college. I don't know what happened, but it sounds like he became depressed when he was up there. I don't really know any details about it, because Mom and Dad stop talking about it when I walk in the room. I only know what little I do because I've been trying to listen in on their conversations. They won't talk about it in front of me.

He was actually a really cool big brother. I hear some of the other kids talking about their older brothers or sisters, and they sound like jerks. Trev wasn't. He didn't mind me hanging out with him, even when his friends came over. He was nice to my friends too. I mean, it wasn't perfect. We had arguments and stuff, but for the most part, he was just a nice, normal guy.

He taught me how to play video games. His favorite game is – *was* – his favorite game was Overwatch. It's so hard to talk about him in the past tense. Anyway, he was a master at playing that game. I liked to just sit and watch him play sometimes. Especially when he played the character, Lucio. Lucio does this thing called "Wall Riding," where he runs and jumps on the tops of buildings and walls, and it's freaking HARD. But, Trev, man... he was the best! There's this one achievement called "The Floor is Lava," and you have to Wall Ride and stay off the ground while getting three kills without falling or getting killed yourself. It's the rarest achievement in the game, and he got it. He had, like, 75% of the achievements in the game, which is amazing. He totally could have gotten to 100% – if he were still here.

Anyway, even though he was so good at the game, he still took the time to help me learn how to play. Sometimes I would play a character while he played a monkey character called Winston, and he would make Winston dance around and stuff just to make me laugh.

He was so funny. He was the funniest person I know. He used to do these goofy ballet kinds of jumps where he would leap as high into the air as he could with his knees out and the bottoms of his feet together and his arms all flung about, and when he was in the air, he would let a loud fart. He called it the Buttcracker Suite. Sometimes he would walk into whatever room Mom was in, and he would just stare at her until she looked up, and she would say, "What's wrong, Trev?" And he would leap and fart, then dance out of the room on his toes. She would yell, "Trevor! Really?!" But we could hear her laughing from the next room.

The thing he was best at though, even better than he was at video games and farting (I know most people don't truly appreciate the skill it takes to do a perfectly timed fart ballet, but gimme a break. I'm in middle school. All middle school boys find farts hilarious.) was climbing. He was an *amazing* rock climber. Mom always talks about how Trevor was climbing before he could even walk.

She couldn't leave him alone, even just to go to the bathroom, because when she would come out, he would be on the back of the couch or on top of the dining room table. He could just pull himself up on anything. When she would tell that story, he would always joke about how he didn't need to be reminded about having to watch her go to the bathroom all the time, and Mom would laugh really hard.

I've always been afraid of heights, but not Trev. He had zero fear. I would go to the climbing gym with him sometimes, and I would pretty much always just be on the low bouldering walls, working super hard just to hang on, while Trev would be crawling up the highest wall in the gym. He was strong and his movements were smooth. People would stop climbing and watch him. Other climbers would ask him for advice or help, and he was always willing to give it.

When he would see buildings made with rocks, or big trees with lots of branches, he would look at Mom and say,

11

"I'll bet I could climb that," and Mom would reply, "Yes, I'm sure you could, Trev, but please don't," and he'd smile and shake his head.

5

The good thing about today was that I got to stay home from school again. The bad thing about today was that I stayed home because I had to go see a therapist.

It was weird. I know Mom and Dad already talked to him because he was asking me about when I ran away from school, and he wanted to know why I ran to the warehouse. I just shrugged my shoulders, and told him I didn't know why I did it. Even if I did know, I wasn't going to tell him. I don't even know him. I don't get why I'm supposed to open up to some stranger, when I can't even talk to my own parents about it.

We can't talk about the one thing that we all can't stop thinking about. I say his name, and Mom starts crying, and Dad gets quiet. I mean... I get it. I know they're sad, but so am I.

And you know what? So was Trevor. I wonder if he felt like he couldn't talk about how he was feeling too.

One day I heard them saying how they were afraid that talking about it in front of me would be too upsetting. That they needed to protect me. Protect me? From what? Thinking about him? Being reminded about what he did? Not talking about him isn't going to protect me from anything. It's not like I'm going to be reminded about what happened. How can you be reminded about something that you can't stop thinking about?

Sometimes I do forget though. Wait – that's not exactly the right word. I just… I guess I still do stuff out of habit, if that makes sense. Like, I started to text him a YouTube video of a goat that was yelling and spitting in this guy's face. I pulled up his number, then remembered he was gone. When stuff like that happens, it's like finding out all over again.

Sometimes I just sit there re-reading our texts to each other, trying to see if I missed something I should have seen. Anything that would have given me any kind of hint that he was thinking of killing himself. Nothing. There was nothing there. It was all just *normal*. I don't know if that made me feel better or worse.

The therapist said I still needed to take another couple of days or so off of school, so at least I feel like he was right about that.

After I left therapy today, I really started trying to figure out why I went to the warehouse, and I think it makes a little more sense to me now. I wanted to go see where it happened. I *needed* to go, but I was afraid to ask. I was afraid of upsetting Mom and Dad. Afraid they would think it was weird or creepy or whatever. Maybe it is. I wouldn't know. I can't freaking talk about it.

I've seen the place before. Lots of times. But I wanted to see what it felt like now, if it felt – I don't know – different, I guess. I wanted to picture the climbing route he took to get to the top. I have watched him climb so many times, I could see him climbing it in my head. I pictured him sticking his fingers in the chain link fence, and once he got up to the barbed wire around the top, I could see him putting his hands between the barbs, and lifting his legs over, and climbing down the other side. Then there was some low pipework on the bottom right corner of the building. He could have used that to get up to the little metal awning above the door. He probably stood on that, and reached the small balcony on the second floor. From there, he could just go from balcony to balcony all the way up to the roof. The thought of trying to do that myself made my stomach do a flip, but I couldn't help but think about going up there with him. What if I had been there that day? What if I had followed him up through the climb, just so he wouldn't feel alone? Maybe if he knew I loved him enough to conquer my fear of heights in order to do that for him, he would have known how much he meant to me. Maybe he wouldn't have left.

6

I've been reading a lot about suicide on the computer
while I've been pretending to do my work for school. I clear
my browser history so Mom and Dad don't see it and think I'm
suicidal too.

Trev is actually the one who taught me how to clear my
browser history back when I was in fourth grade. I had
overheard a kid at school say the word "cock" and the other
kids laughed. I didn't know what it meant, but I knew it had to
be something bad. I was embarrassed to ask Mom and Dad, so
I Googled it. I clicked on "images," and all I saw was some
pictures of roosters, and I knew that couldn't be right, so I
poked around, and figured out how to turn off the Safe Search
and tried again, and… ummm… yeah. The next thing I knew, I
was looking at a bunch of penises. Row after row of dicks. I
panicked and closed it down, and went back to my room. Later

that evening, Mom and Dad knocked on my door and said we needed to have a talk. They shut the door and sat down all serious-like, and asked me if I thought I was attracted to dudes. At first, I was too shocked and embarrassed to say anything, then I remembered all those dicks and realized why they were asking. But before I could explain what had happened, Mom thought my silence meant they were right, and she was already telling me that it was okay, and that they would love and support me no matter who I fell in love with, and I yelled, "Mom! No! I heard someone say *cock* today at school, and I was trying to figure out what it meant!" They both said, "Oh!" like, almost at the same time, and Mom awkwardly patted me on the knee, and they left the room.

I was humiliated.

Trev came in a few minutes later to see what happened, but instead of making fun of me, he showed me how to clear my search history. He said that way I could look at cocks all day long if I wanted to, and no one would know. The way he said it made me realize how funny it really was, and the next thing I knew, we were both laughing so hard we were crying.

He took the most embarrassing moment of my life, and made it one of my funniest memories.

7

Mom and Dad brought me into the living room to have

a talk after Dad got home from work. I thought we were finally

going to talk about what happened to Trevor, but I was wrong.

They told me they think I need to go back to see the therapist

again. I got pretty upset, and told them that I didn't want to go.

I said that it made me feel weird to talk to a stranger about

something that I couldn't even talk to them about.

They both just sat there and stared at me in shock. I was

waiting for Mom to start crying again, but this time it was Dad.

I couldn't believe it. He was always the one who comforted me

and Mom when we cried. I knew he cried too though, because

he would come out of his room or the bathroom sometimes,

and his eyes would be all red and puffy, so to see him break

down in front of me made me feel like crying, too. I scooted over next to him and hugged him and cried. Then Mom went and got tissues, and she joined in. We all just sat there having a big old blubber-fest for a few minutes.

It sounds super weird, but it was such a relief. I could tell they were relieved too. They asked me what I wanted to know, so I asked them if Trevor left a note. I knew from stuff I had read before, and like, when someone on TV does it, sometimes they write a note explaining why they did it, and it seemed to make people feel better to know it wasn't their fault. But Mom said no. He hadn't left a note, and we would probably never know why he did it.

I felt sick when I heard that. I was scared to hear what he said in the note, but now I would never know whether or not it was my fault.

I feel plenty guilty when I think about how when he left for college, I was excited. I mean, of course I knew I would miss him, but I really wanted his room. It was bigger than mine, and farther away from Mom and Dad's room, so as soon as he was out, I was moving my stuff in.

I also didn't know what to do when he came home and he was acting differently. I knew he was depressed, but I didn't know how to talk to him, so I just… didn't. Here I was taking over his room, and just sort of ignoring him while he was struggling. The more I thought about it, the more I believed I was right. I failed him. It may not have been totally because of me, but I sure didn't help things any. If I could go back and do it again, I would never have taken his room, and I would have tried talking to him more and stuff.

I was scared to tell Mom and Dad, because I thought they would be upset with me, but I couldn't stand it any longer. I told them everything about how it was my fault.

Mom and Dad both listened, then they said that they felt guilty too, and that they *"what if?"* all the time, and that they would give anything for a do-over. They worried they didn't do enough, or maybe they did too much. Dad said the real reason had nothing to do with any of us. He was just sick. His brain was sick, and he wasn't seeing things clearly. We couldn't fix Trev, because we weren't what was wrong with Trev.

It makes sense. I mean, it's like I know that in my head, but my heart... my heart feels different.

"It's as if your head and your heart aren't on the same page," Mom said.

"Or even in the same book," Dad added.

Exactly. That's exactly it.

When we were done talking, and it was time for bed, for the first time in forever, Dad followed me upstairs and tucked me in. He sat on the edge of my bed and said he was sorry for the mistakes he and Mom made with me when Trev died. I told him I understood, and that it's just really hard. He nodded his head, and said, "Yes. Yes, it is. I don't know how to do this."

8

I went in to visit the school counselor today to talk to him about going back to school. He seemed pretty surprised that I was doing what he told me I should do with the journal thing, and he asked me if I thought it was helping. I really thought about it, and I realized it felt like it was. It doesn't feel as weird anymore. I almost look forward to it now.

Mr. Blackwell told me that he was really sad when he heard that Trevor had died. He was a counselor there when Trev was in middle school, and he remembered him and really liked him. It made me feel good to know that out of all the students he sees year after year, he remembered my brother.

He said that when Trev was my age, there was a boy in his class named Jimmy. Jimmy had mild cerebral palsy. He could walk and talk and stuff, and he was a really nice guy, but some of the kids made fun of him and didn't want to hang out with him. Trev and a few boys were hanging around outside during their lunch break, and they were playing some stupid game where they would steal one kid's hat, and try to keep it away from him. Jimmy came running up and took the hat, but when he did it, one of the kids pushed him down. He said Trev just lost it, and knocked the kid down, got down on the ground, and punched him in the face. Mr. Blackwell said he and the principal had a long, serious talk with Trev about how violence isn't the answer to anything, including bullying, and they gave him after-school detention because they had to give him some type of punishment, but deep inside, they were both really proud of him for standing up for Jimmy.

It made me proud too.

He also said there are lots of theories as to why someone decides to kill themselves, but one of them is that people who try it feel things differently than other people. He said they have more empathy. I didn't really understand what that meant, but the way he explained it, I think that *sympathy* is when you feel sorry for someone else. Like if someone gets bullied, you feel bad that they feel bad, but *empathy* is when you feel more than sorry. Like, you truly feel the same emotion they feel. He said the story he had just told me was the first thing he thought of when he heard about Trev. He had freaked out and punched his friend because he could feel the fear and sadness that Jimmy was feeling in that moment. Maybe he had too much empathy.

I can't stop thinking about that – about how hard it would be to see all of the awful, hurtful things that people do to each other all the time, and not be able to stop feeling what they were feeling. I wouldn't want to get out of bed either.

Mr. Blackwell and I decided I should give school another try tomorrow. Now that I know what to expect, hopefully it will be a little easier to just ignore the looks. He also said I would probably have trouble focusing, and I shouldn't worry about it too much. Just to do my best, and if I need to leave the classroom, I could just quietly get up and come to his office.

I'm so glad he said that, because one of the reasons that I was scared to go back was that I felt like I would be stuck in class with everyone watching me if I cried. Now I know I can leave class, and have someplace to go.

9

I hadn't heard much from any of my friends while I was home from school. I mean, I don't really have a lot of friends. Just a few, actually. It's not like I wish I was popular or anything. I have a lot of different people that I talk to in classes and stuff, and nobody picks on me or anything like that. But as far as hanging out, I usually just want to be with my best friend, Ryan. I was worried that things would be weird with him when I went back to school, because I haven't heard much from him since Trev died. It kind of hurts my feelings, to be honest, but at the same time, when I think about what I would do if it was his brother, Kyle, I don't know what I would say to him either. It's weird. I'm right in the middle of it, but I still don't think I would know how to help somebody else who was going through the same thing. Like, I don't think there's anything you can say to make things better, you know?

When I got to school this morning, I put my earbuds in as I walked to class. I didn't turn any music on, but I could pretty much ignore people and pretend that I was totally into my music and not just avoiding them. We're not allowed to wear them in the classroom. We can't even have our phones out of our backpacks or pockets unless the teacher says we can take them out to photograph the whiteboard for assignments. When I got to the classroom, my heart was pounding again, and I was pretty nervous, but I looked down at the floor, and didn't make eye contact with anyone. Mrs. McKay didn't welcome me back or anything, so it was a little less weird. I finally got my notebook and pencil out, and I turned to look across the room to see if Ryan was there, and he was looking at me. He gave me a "Bro Nod," and I gave one back, which made both of us laugh a little, and it felt normal. He acted like he was eating something to let me know he would save me a seat at lunch, because his fourth period classroom was closer to the cafeteria than mine.

My classes were pretty normal. Mr. B was right about my focus. I couldn't really concentrate on what was going on, but I guess I expected that. A few of the kids told me that they were sorry to hear about my brother. I don't know what I'm supposed to say to that. Mom and Dad say "thank you" when people say that, but that seems weird to me. What are they thanking people for? Thank you for feeling sorry for me? I just say, "me too" because I am. I am sorry he's gone. I don't know if that's right or not, but it's how I feel about it. And sometimes I just nod, because if I try to say anything at all, I get all choked up.

At lunch time, I found Ryan where we always sit. I sat down, and he said, "I'm glad you're back. I've had to sit with Kevin every day." Kevin isn't a bad guy, but you have to keep your food away from him. You have to put it in your lap, or on the bench next to you, because if you put it all on the table where he can reach it, he will help himself to everything. There were never leftovers when you sat with Kevin.

It got quiet for a bit, then he told me he was sorry that he didn't text very much, but he just didn't know what to say.

Ryan said he was really upset to hear about Trevor. That he was always really nice to him, and he was thinking about how funny he was, and how it just didn't make sense that he would do what he did. His eyes started to water, which made my eyes water, and neither one of us wanted to cry at the table, so I just pulled my brownie out of my bag and broke it in two, and handed half to him. He pulled four Oreos out of his bag, and handed me two. At lunch we always shared our dessert, and we always ate it first. It was a relief to do something normal.

10

Today was my second day back at school. People didn't seem as weird around me today. It's like they got all of the stares and stuff out of the way yesterday. One thing I did notice is that the things they talk about and worry about seem more – I don't know – just... stupid, I guess. I overheard two guys talking about how bad it sucked that they didn't have ranch for the chicken nuggets in the cafeteria today. Like, they were furious. They kept saying things like, "This SUCKS! I can't eat nuggets without ranch! Why didn't they tell us they were out when I chose nuggets?" They were freaking out over ranch dressing. I was sitting there thinking about how stupid it was to get so upset about it, then I remembered a couple of months ago when it was pizza day and Ryan and I brought money to buy lunch, but they didn't have pepperoni pizza. It was just cheese. We did the same thing the other two guys were doing. We freaked out over pepperoni. It's weird. It's really hard for me not to get pissed about the dumb stuff people get worked up over, even though it's the same dumb stuff that I used to complain about. It makes me wish that I could go back to when not having pepperoni on pizza was the worst thing that might happen to me.

A group of girls was talking before English class started, and a girl named Tasha said she had tried out for the school play. She was complaining about how she never gets to be the lead, and she said, "If I don't get cast as Jasmine, I'm gonna kill myself." The girl next to her cleared her throat, and glanced my way, and Tasha turned around and looked at me, and I could tell she felt really bad. She said, "I'm so sorry, Cody... I didn't think." I sort of mumbled, "I know. It's okay." I was trying to just blow it off, but the more I thought about it, the more I felt like I was going to cry. I got up as the bell rang, and I went to Mrs. Corte's desk, and said I needed to go see

Mr. Blackwell, and she quickly wrote up a slip without saying a word.

I sat in his office and cried for a while, and he let me. I cried so hard I got the hiccups. He didn't ask what had happened until I stopped. Then I told him, and somehow through my sniffling and hiccupping, he seemed to understand most of what I was saying. Mr. B talked about how there were words and phrases that used to be accepted that aren't any more, because they're hurtful and offensive. People used to say stuff was "gay" as an insult, or that people were "retarded," and we don't say those things any more. He said it was time to stop people from saying that they would kill themselves, because it made it into a joke, and it's not. I've even heard adults say it. I hadn't ever really thought about it much, but now that my brother killed himself, I realize how awful it sounds. And, like, it's even awful for the person saying it, too, you know? Like their life is only worth some stupid part in a middle school play.

I stayed in his office until the bell rang, and then I got up to go. When I stepped into the hall, Tasha was there waiting for me, and

I could see that she had been crying. She said she was sorry again, and that she didn't mean to hurt my feelings. She handed me my backpack, and said she took a pic of the assignment on the whiteboard and would send it to me if I gave her my phone number. I'm not gonna lie. I've thought a lot about how cool it would be to have a girl want my number so we could text each other, but this definitely wasn't the way I pictured it happening.

11

I got some of my make-up work back from school today. I didn't do so great. I usually make A's and B's without really trying, but I don't know... I just can't seem to make myself care. I mean, I can do the work, but I don't want to. I can't really concentrate on it anyway, but it's more than that. It just seems pointless. Trevor studied, got good grades, got into the college he wanted to go to and, well, you know what happened. What if that happens to me too? I've been reading about it, and I read that big transitions, or like, traumatic events can trigger depression and suicide. I'm kind of scared about it. He was just such a... a normal guy before. He did okay in school. I mean, he wasn't super popular, but he had friends. He made the same grades I do. I keep thinking back to try to figure out if there was something that I missed. Something that would make it make some sense, but there's nothing. He would get sad about stuff, sure. Like he had a girlfriend who broke up with him, and he was pretty bummed about that, but I think everyone that gets dumped feels bad about it. And he didn't stay that way. I think sadness is different from depression, you know? Like sadness is an emotion. You feel it when there's a reason for it. Depression is when everything in your life is going okay, but you still feel like it's not, and like it won't get better.

I went into Trev's room today. His door has been shut since he died. I thought about sneaking in there, but I went ahead and asked Mom if I could just sit in there with his stuff. She said I could go in there any time I wanted. Of course, it used to be my room, but all of his stuff was in there now, and nothing had changed since he walked out the door that day. His bed was still unmade, like he had just slept in it. I know it sounds weird, but I went over and sat down on it, and I could smell him. I didn't even really notice that he had a smell until now, but it was super weird how much it made me remember him. I closed my eyes and I could picture him lying on his back with his earbuds in, and his knee bent up with his other ankle resting on it. His foot bouncing to the beat of the song he was listening to. Probably Deadmau5. That was one of his favorite bands. I opened my eyes, and of course he wasn't there, and for some reason it felt like I had lost him all over again. I laid down with my head on his pillow, and just looked around his room.

As I was lying there, I looked over and saw his backpack on the floor. I went over and opened it up and pulled out a notebook. The cover said, "ENG 150 – Creative Writing Journal." I turned some pages, and there were only a few with writing on them. I turned to the last one, and all it said was, "People always ask me if I'm afraid of falling when I climb, and I say no. What I don't tell them is that falling doesn't scare me at all. What really scares me is that I want to jump."

12

I'm worried about Mom. She's not really eating anything, and her clothes look loose and baggy on her. I've been watching, and she just moves her food around on her plate like I do when I don't want to eat my peas. She always looks at me and says, "You're not fooling anyone, Cody."

You're not fooling anyone either, Mom.

When I see her like this, I get pissed. Not at Mom, but at Trevor. I mean, we are all upset about him, but I feel like it's making Mom sick, like physically, you know? I don't understand how he could do this to her. How could he not know or care that it was going to be so awful for her? I heard her on the phone with Grandma, and she said she felt like she was living in a nightmare, but she can't wake up.

I feel really guilty for being mad at him, but I can't help it. I talked to Mr. B about it, and he said that it was normal for me to feel that way. That really anything I feel right now would be pretty normal, because I'm grieving. Grief makes you feel different things at different times, and that even if I have a good day, I might think I'm better, but the next day could be bad again. He said that it isn't like walking a straight line, but it takes you all over the place, like a roller coaster that sometimes goes backwards. It's curvy and hilly and complicated.

When I asked him how Trevor could leave us and not know how much it would hurt us, he said that he had a student one time who tried to die by suicide, but he survived. He told Mr. B that he felt like his brain was lying to him. He said that he knew he was loved, but he didn't understand why. That he felt like he wasn't deserving of their love, and that they would be better off without him. He felt like it was going to make things easier for his family and friends if he wasn't around anymore.

"He was sick, Cody," Mr. B said, "Just like someone who has diabetes, or a heart problem. His brain wasn't working properly."

I wish they would call mental illness a brain disease, because I think that's what it is. When people talk about mental illness, it makes you think, "Oh, they're crazy," which sounds bad. I hear people all the time asking other people if they're "mental" when they do something weird or whatever.

I don't know if I'm explaining it right, but if someone had like a tumor or something in their brain, people would feel bad for them… but when people talk about someone having a mental illness, it's like they're making fun, you know? Like they point their finger at their head and make circles. They say things like, "their elevator doesn't reach the top floor" or "they're a few French fries short of a Happy Meal." Sure, it sounds funny, but it's not. It's not funny at all, and it makes it hard for someone who has a brain disorder to ask for help or tell anyone about it. It sucks.

When I think about Trev feeling sad and alone, and like he didn't have any hope, but he was embarrassed to ask for help, I can't feel mad at him anymore. It must have been so awful for him to feel like something was wrong, but to be ashamed of it.

13

Today at school, Ryan invited me over to his house on Saturday. I was pumped to get home and ask if I could go, but when I walked in the door, I knew something was wrong. Mom's eyes were all red, and Dad was already home. I asked what was wrong, and he said that they just got home from picking up Trev's ashes.

I didn't know how to feel. I mean, there was just something about having his ashes that made it feel real. Like he was really gone. I looked over, and there was a big, brown plastic box on the table. I dropped my backpack, and walked over to look at it. There was a label that said:

HERITAGE CREMATORY
Herein lies the cremated remains of:
MITCHELL, Trevor Warren
Date of Birth: July 22, 1999
Date of Death: January, 25, 2018
Cremated on: February 6, 2018

It made my stomach feel queasy, and I got dizzy, and I

had to sit down. I'd heard Mom and Dad talking about the

ambulance... trauma... police... remains... coroner...

autopsy... but it felt like they were talking about someone else.

Like it was one of those CSI TV shows or something. I

couldn't stand to think of any of it happening to Trevor, so I

didn't. But, seeing his ashes there on the table, I just... I

couldn't picture it before, but now I couldn't stop picturing it.

It was like a movie in my head.

Trevor on the roof. Backing up. Running to the edge.

Jumping. Hitting the ground. Sirens. Police. Ambulance.

Hospital. All those tubes, and people in masks trying to save

him... My ears started rushing, and my chest was hurting, and I

couldn't get a deep breath. Mom had my face in her hands, and

I could see her saying my name, and looking scared, but I

couldn't say anything. I finally saw that she was saying, "Look

at me! Look at me, Cody! Breathe... deep breath... You're

okay..." I was finally able to catch my breath, and Dad brought

me a glass of water. Mom said, "I think you just had a panic

attack. Are you okay now? Can you breathe?" I could. I was

calming down, but I felt, I don't know, empty. Hollow. I felt like I did the morning after I went to a sleepover, and we stayed up all night. I felt lightheaded and sick at my stomach, and I could feel my heartbeat in my chest all fluttery and fast.

I had been feeling a little better, but I felt almost as bad now than I did when I first found out he had died. I laid down on the couch, and closed my eyes for a minute, but I guess I fell asleep, because when I opened my eyes, the sky was darker than it had been, and I didn't know how long I had been there. Mom and Dad were sitting in the room with me, and they asked how I was feeling. They said I had slept for a couple of hours. Mom didn't feel like cooking, so they ordered pizza. My stomach growled when I smelled it. I felt better after eating a couple of slices.

I asked them why his ashes were in a box instead of one of those jar things that I couldn't remember the name of. Mom said it was an urn. I remembered that was the word after she said it. Dad said they didn't see any that they really liked, or that really fit Trev's personality, so they were going to look online for one. I sat for a minute and thought about it, then I had an idea.

When we were both babies, our uncle made each of us a wooden keepsake box that we put our favorite things in. Trev's was sitting on his dresser. I asked if maybe we could use it for his ashes. Mom and Dad looked at each other in surprise, and they said it would be perfect. They brought the box in, and we all sat around and went through his things together. There was a two-dollar bill, one of those gold Sacagawea coins, his class ring and tassel from his graduation cap, some photos and stuff. Then we found Briefcase Man. When Trev was little, he liked train sets, and he collected tiny people and trees and buildings for his train set up. His favorite thing though, was Briefcase Man. He never named him for some reason. He was in a black suit, with a black hat and sunglasses, and he was holding a briefcase. He looked like a tiny Blues Brother. The only thing that moved on him was his arms. Trevor carried him everywhere. Mom was always digging him out of Trev's pockets when she did laundry. We all thought he had gotten lost, but there he was. We decided to put him back in the box with Trev's ashes, because that's where he really belonged. I know it sounds weird, but I felt a little better knowing that he wasn't alone in there. Trevor was back home with us now, and he had his favorite thing.

14

Mom wasn't sure if I should go back to school after yesterday, but I was still pretty behind and just not doing very well in my classes, so I felt like I shouldn't miss again. She said I could go back if I would talk to Mr. Blackwell before class. I agreed it was probably a good idea. I felt like he was helping me. He was pretty much the one person I could say anything to, and not have to worry about it. I told her about Ryan inviting me over, and she said if today went okay, and I felt like going, I could.

I told Mr. B what happened yesterday, and he said it made sense that it was so upsetting. He said that when someone has a traumatic loss like this, that's totally unexpected, it's like it's too much for your brain to deal with all at once, so it just deals with little bits of it at a time, and that's how people live in denial. Coming home and seeing his ashes made it all real, and it was just too much to take in.

It makes my stomach hurt to think of him being burned up into ashes. When Mom and Dad were talking about it, Mom said she couldn't stand to think of him all alone in a cemetery. She wanted him home. I think both options pretty much suck. I can't stand to think of my big brother in a grave *or* burned up in a box on a shelf. I know that people will sometimes scatter some of the ashes in their favorite place. It might be nice to do that. He always liked the warehouse. We used to ride our bikes there all the time. There were stray cats that hung out there, and when we brought Trev home from college, and he felt good enough to come out of his room, we went and found out that one of them had three kittens. We started taking food to them, and we gave them names. There was a striped one that we named Kevin, because he tried to eat everyone else's food. We named the little gray and white one Wilbern. He was named after my grandpa, because he had gray fur. And there was a calico that we named Berniece. Actually, we didn't know whether or not they were boys or girls, except for Berniece. We knew she was a girl, because Trev learned in science class that all calico cats are female. She was named after my grandma. We had gotten to the point where they would come to the food if we were standing a few feet away, and we were trying to get to where we could pet them. We were so close. None of the bigger cats would come near us, but the kittens seemed to be more used to us. They wouldn't let us pet them, but they weren't quite as spazzy as the bigger cats. I need to go back there and see how they're doing. I haven't been back since I ran there after school. I hope they haven't been too hungry.

The rest of the school day was okay, I guess. I still can't concentrate, but I don't know what to do about it. I catch myself daydreaming, then I panic, then I can't stop thinking about what I missed, so I can't think about the new stuff the teacher is saying, either.

When the final bell rang, I walked out into the hall, and saw a bunch of kids reading the bulletin board. It was the cast list for Aladdin. I squeezed through the group to read it, and the first thing I saw was, "Jasmine – Jessica Cunningham." I looked for Tasha's name, and there it was: Iago. It seemed like a pretty good part to me, so I hoped that she was happy about it. I looked around for her, but I guess she already left.

During dinner I talked to Mom and Dad about my day, and about seeing Mr. B, and they both said it was okay for me to go to Ryan's tomorrow. I went straight to my room to let him know I was coming over. Then I stared at my phone. I was trying to decide if I should text Tasha to congratulate her on her part, and to see if she was okay. She has been talking to me more at school and stuff, but I didn't want her to think I liked her. I mean, I do. I *like her* like her, you know? I pulled up her number and typed, "Congratulations on your role!" Then I deleted it. What if she wasn't happy about it? So I typed, "Sorry you didn't get cast as Jasmine." *Nope.* She might be okay with Iago, and if I say I'm sorry about it, she might think I don't think it's a good role. I deleted that too, then typed, "Hey! I saw the cast list, and wanted to tell you how cool it is that you are going to get to be Iago. He's one of my favorite characters from the movie." Then I sent it. Then I waited. I got an immediate notification… from Ryan. My phone dinged again, and it was her. I could feel my heart pounding. She replied, "Thank you, Cody. That's really sweet."

Yes! Then another ding… "Do you think it's weird that I'll be playing a part that's supposed to be for a guy?"

I sent back, "No way! I think it's cool! Jasmine is really boring. Iago is way funnier."

She sent, "You're right. I think Iago is more fun too. I had fun reading it at the audition, but I guess I'm just afraid that I got the part because I'm not pretty enough to play Jasmine."

Uh oh… Oh crap, I didn't know what to say. I mean, I do think she's pretty. She doesn't look like Jessica, who is, like, cheerleader pretty. But Jessica also looks mean, especially when she's not smiling. Ryan says she has Resting Bitch Face. He learned that from his brother. We've learned *a lot* of horrible things from his brother. Tasha doesn't look scary when she's not smiling, and when she is smiling… well, she has a great smile. So, I think she's way prettier than Jessica, but should I tell her that? I needed to say something quick, because I knew she was waiting for a response, and if I waited too long she might think I agree with her. Holy crap, this is so hard! I quickly typed, "Sorry about making you wait. I had to go to the bathroom." Oh god, no! *Delete.* okay…

"You are more than pretty enough to play Jasmine, but I think it's harder to play Iago. Mrs. Araujo must think you're a better actress than Jessica." Send. And wait.

She sent back a GIF of Iago dancing, and "Thank you, Cody! I feel so much better about it now!" with a heart emoji. *A heart emoji!*

Holy crap.

15

Mom dropped me off at Ryan's house and his brother, Kyle, answered the door. I got ready for him to call me some horrible name that I'd have to look up later on Urban Dictionary. He had a new creative name each time he saw me. Last time I saw him, he called me Penis Wrinkle.

I didn't have to look that one up.

Not today, though. Today he said, "Hey, little dude, come on in. Ry's in the game room."

I stared at him in shock, then I mumbled, "Ummm... Thanks?"

As I walked past him, he said, "Yo, little dude. I was, like, totally bummed to hear about Trev, man. He was all right."

"Yeah," I said. "He was."

It was the longest conversation I've ever had with Kyle. He was usually a total douche canoe. (That was one of the first ones I learned from him.)

Ryan and I played video games, plowed through a family sized bag of Doritos, ate his mom's homemade spaghetti, watched YouTube videos of people wiping out – and I told him about my texts from Tasha.

It was the most normal and fun thing I've done since Trev died. We didn't even talk about him at all.

And now I feel like crap.

I feel guilty for not thinking about him. I feel guilty for having fun while he won't be able to ever do anything fun again. That, like, if he can see me or whatever, and I was laughing and stuff, he might feel bad. Like I've forgotten about him.

I talked to Dad about it a little bit when I got home, and he said that he feels guilty for thinking of other things too, but then he thinks about what Trev would have wanted, and that he would want him to be happy, and he would want me to be happy too.

I said I agreed, but I don't know if I do. I don't feel like I really know who he was anymore. It feels like my big brother went off to college, and a stranger came back in his place. The Trevor that I know would never have wanted to die.

In the middle of his first semester of college, Mom told me Trevor was depressed, and that Dad was going to bring him home. I felt bad that he was sad, but I didn't really understand how depression is different than sadness. I thought maybe he was homesick, and he would feel better being back home.

He put his stuff in my old room, and pretty much just stayed there. He was… quiet. Mom or Dad would have to go get him for meals, and for his therapy appointments, and to give him his medicine, but other than that, he pretty much just stayed in bed. Sometimes they would make him go outside to get some fresh air, but he would just sit there in a chair with his elbows on his knees, and his head in his hands.

Any time he came out of his room, he looked like he had been asleep. His hair wasn't washed, and he never got out of his pajamas. Mom brought him out to the dining room and made all of his favorite foods, like steak, and homemade mac-n-cheese and cheesecake, but he wouldn't even pretend to move it around on his plate.

One day, Mom did some laundry, and she asked me to take Trev's clean clothes to him, so I went into his room, and he was lying on his side, facing me. He was awake, so I asked him where he wanted his stuff.

He said, "I don't care." I laid the stuff on his dresser and asked him if he wanted to play Overwatch, and he said, "No."

I said, "Okay," and started to walk out.

He added, "I'm sorry. None of the things I used to like to do make me happy any more. Nothing works."

I said, "I'm really sorry, Trev. Maybe the medicine will start making you feel better soon."

He didn't reply. He just closed his eyes, so I walked out and closed the door.

A couple of days later, he came out of his room on his own. He sat down on the couch, and started playing Overwatch. I went out and got Mom and Dad, and we all just sat with him, and watched him play. We were smiling at each other and Mom was getting all teary eyed.

It felt good.

It felt like hope.

16

Today at lunch, I went to sit with Ryan in our regular

place, and Tasha and her best friend Keziah were sitting across

from him. He looked pretty panicked. I sat next to him, and

said hi to everyone. I wasn't sure what else to say, so I pulled

my chocolate chip cookies out of my bag. I had two, so I

handed one to Ryan, and he handed me two peanut butter

Oreos. The girls just stared at us. Keziah asked us what we

were doing, and when we told them, they immediately smiled

and dug their desserts out of their lunch bags. Keziah suggested

we split everything four ways, so we could get a little bit of

each. We agreed that it was a brilliant idea, because it meant I

got to add a Nutter Butter and a couple of Thin Mints to my

stash. We all started talking about what our favorite school lunch desserts were while we ate, and it wasn't awkward any more. It was just... nice.

When I got home, I asked Mom if we could get some of those little powdered sugar donuts for my school lunch dessert, and she said it was no problem, and asked what made me decide that I wanted them since I've never been interested in them before. I told her that they were my friend Tasha's favorite, and that we shared our desserts today.

Mom said, "You want to take donuts to a girl?" And she looked so happy. Happier than I've seen her look in weeks. Then she got all teary, and came over and hugged me, and said that it was nice to see me doing normal things like having a crush on a girl and taking her a treat, and that she would have loved that when she was that age. I wanted to argue that I didn't have a crush on her because I was embarrassed, but I was also kind of glad to tell her. I mean, I did have a crush on her- and it was weird to think of Mom at that age, but good to know that girls like the sort of thing I was planning on doing. I'm also betting that she was relieved that she didn't have to worry about me taking donuts to school for a dude. I imagine finding all those penises in your 9-year-old son's search history is an image that would stay with you for quite some time.

I just wish Trevor was here for me to talk to about it. Usually my feelings about what he did are all mixed up, and it's hard to really know what I'm feeling. It's like when sometimes my mom will bring me a jumble of her necklaces so I can untangle the one she wants to wear. They're all wrapped around each other, and when you try to separate them, it's almost impossible. All my emotions are usually in a big knot when it comes to Trev's suicide. Not tonight though. Tonight, there's only one thing I'm feeling: tonight, I just miss him.

I recorded this update in his room, because it's the closest I can get to him.

17

Last night I dreamed about Trevor. I've read about people having what they call "visitations" from people that have died. They dream about seeing them and talking to them, and it makes them feel better. It wasn't like that for me. I dreamed that we were looking for him, and I got on my bike to go find him, because I knew he was probably at the warehouse, but when I tried to ride, my bike broke in half. I started to run, but it felt like I could only move in slow motion and when I looked around, I didn't recognize where I was, so I didn't know how to get there to save him. I knew he needed me, but I couldn't do anything to help him. I hope it wasn't a visitation dream because if it was, he was telling me that I wasn't there when he needed me in real life. I woke up and couldn't go back to sleep for a long time.

I went to school a little early so I could talk to Mr. B. He said that the dream wasn't Trev trying to send me a message or anything like that. It was just that, like, deep in my brain, I felt like I should have done more. He was right about that. I do feel that way. I mean, it's hard to explain but, like, I don't feel like it's *all* because of me that he died, but I do feel like maybe I didn't do enough to help him, you know? Mr. B. reminded me that I couldn't have done anything to help him, because he had made up his mind already. I told him it was hard for me to think that way, because he was doing so much better the week before he died. It didn't make sense. Mr. B. said it was common for people who attempt suicide to be positive and act like their old selves before they try it. He said once Trevor had made up his mind that he was going to do it, and he had a plan and knew his pain would be over soon, he felt relieved. It meant he was at peace with his decision. It's scary. I mean, we were all so happy that he was so much better – we didn't even know that was one of the signs. How were we supposed to know that's how it worked? It's all so confusing.

For once, I didn't feel any better when I left his office.

Mom packed donuts for my lunch today, and when I pulled them out of my bag, Tasha was pretty happy. She said, "OMG! You remembered these are my favorite!"

I said, "Well, yeah, I mean, you just told me yesterday."

I didn't want to make a big deal out of it, but I think it made her feel stupid, like she wanted to think I did something nice for her, and I blew if off and made it not such a big deal. It's so hard knowing what to say, and how to act. Mom said to just be myself, but I'm a seventh-grade kid who still thinks farts are funny, and I still look like I'm in elementary school. What if she just likes me as a friend, or if she's just being nice to me because she feels bad for making me feel bad? Like, what if she's my pity friend? And what if she *does* like me? That's actually worse, because what do I do then? I have no idea how to have a girlfriend.

Then I got my last paper back in English class, and I got a D. Mrs. Corte was really cool, and she told me I could rewrite it. Tasha asked me if everything was okay because she saw me looking bummed after talking to the teacher. I told her what happened, and she offered to help me with the rewrite. She said she would ask her mom if she could stay after school tomorrow to help me. I told her I would ask my mom too.

When I got home, I asked Mom about it, and she got all excited, and said, "Why don't you just invite her here for the afternoon?" And before I knew what even happened, she had the school directory out and was on the phone with Tasha's mom, and she was inviting her to come over to the house to do homework and stay for dinner.

I freaked out and said, "Mom, what did you just do?!"

She laughed. My mom *laughed*… like, really laughed for the first time in weeks. I couldn't even stay mad at her.

Holy smokes. Today was a freaking roller coaster.

18

School was okay today. It dragged by, because I was
nervous all day thinking about Tasha coming over, but when
she did, it was really nice. She helped me edit my paper, and it
made a big difference. I was embarrassed by all the mistakes I
had overlooked when I turned it in, but she was totally cool
about it. She said she didn't know how I could think at all
because when she tries to imagine what it would be like if her
sister did what Trevor did, she feels like crying. I told her that's
how I feel a lot of the time. I hadn't even really talked to Ryan
about it too much, but for some reason it was easier to talk to
Tasha about what happened and how it happened. I told her
about how he climbed the outside of the building, and how
someone saw him up there and called the police, but when the
police got there, Trev backed up and then ran and jumped right

in front of them. I told her about how Mom and I were at the grocery store when the hospital called, and we left the shopping cart in the middle of the aisle and ran to the car. We met Dad at the hospital, and we waited for five hours while Trevor was in surgery. It felt like five years. The surgeon came out about halfway through it and said that Trev's feet and ankles were messed up pretty bad, so they had to amputate both of them, and that he had also lost a lot of blood. We were just glad he was alive. I immediately started thinking about how we could put up ramps to make it easy for him to get in the house in a wheelchair, and that we'd move Trev into the downstairs guest bedroom. I was planning how I was going to help him when he came home. A couple of hours later, a lady who worked at the hospital but wasn't a doctor or nurse came to get us, and she took us to a room and told us that the surgeon would be in to talk to us. Mom closed her eyes, and leaned over with her head in her hands while Dad rubbed her back. I heard this high-pitched sound, and I didn't know what it was. Then I realized it was Mom. It was like the sound an animal makes when it's hurt. It didn't even sound like her. I knew it was bad. I knew because Mom knew. I knew because if he was okay, they would come out to talk to us in the waiting room like they did earlier… like they were doing with everybody else in the waiting room. The surgeon came in looking upset, and she still had her mask around her neck, and she was holding her hat in her hands, and it was all wadded up like she'd been twisting it. I could tell she was trying not to cry.

She sat down and said, "We did everything we could, but we lost him."

It was like watching a movie. Mom was crying and saying "no" over and over again, and Dad was trying to calm her down, but he was crying too, and I was just… I don't know, I was just trying to make it make sense somehow.

It was his legs. How could he be dead if he just hurt his legs?! People live without their legs all the time! I guess I was saying it out loud, because the surgeon looked at me and said that his lungs were bleeding, and they couldn't get it to stop. She said they tried everything. They even removed part of one of his lungs. She said she was sorry, then she was crying too.

She asked if we would like to go see him. Mom and Dad immediately said yes, then they looked at me. I was scared, but I did want to see him. We went in and he was just lying there with his eyes closed. He had a big tube in his mouth, but other than that, he just looked like he was sleeping. There were no bruises on his face or anything. I wanted to shake him and wake him up. I wanted to hug him, but I knew he was hurt, and I didn't want to make it worse. It made no sense to me that he was dead. I just stood there and stared at him while Mom and Dad cried and kissed his forehead and rubbed his hair. I finally reached over and put my hand on his face. It was cold, and that's when I knew it was real. That's when I backed away from him into the wall, and my legs wouldn't hold me up anymore. I slid down the wall, and put my head between my knees and sobbed.

When I got to that part of the story, I was bawling and Tasha was too. She said she was sorry, and she hugged me.

While she had her face on my shoulder, she went, "OMG! Oh no!" and she pushed away from me with her hands over her mouth and nose.

I freaked out, and asked, "What? What's wrong?"

She said, "I think I just got snot on your shirt! I'm so sorry! OMG!"

I told her it was okay, and that snot happens when people cry, and if it would make her feel better, I could wipe my nose on her shirt too, and she laughed.

She asked me if she could see a picture of Trev. His graduation picture was on a shelf in the living room, so I took her out there and showed it to her. She said he was handsome, and that we looked alike. I went to the computer and brought up more pictures, and Mom came in to check on us, and we all ended up looking at pictures and telling stories about him for almost an hour. Tasha asked if we would mind if she went to the warehouse with us some time to put flowers there for him. I said Trev wasn't really a flowers kind of guy, but maybe we could go feed Wilbern, Berniece and Kevin. Mom said Trev would have loved that, and she would get some cat food and take us over there on Saturday if it was okay with Tasha's mom.

It was weird to talk about all of that, but it's the first time I've told anyone everything, and it was such a relief. I mean, it seems like no one else wants to talk about him or what happened, and I spilled my guts to Tasha about it, and instead of being awkward or weird, she wanted to know even more about him. It feels good to talk about him. I don't want people to forget him, you know?

It also makes me feel less scared of her. Especially since she snotted on me.

19

At school today, a couple of eighth graders came up to me in the cafeteria, and one of them asked if I was the kid whose brother committed suicide.

I said, "My brother *died* from suicide. He didn't *commit* anything."

So he goes, "Whatever, dude."

Then the other kid said, "How did he do it? Someone said he hung himself in the garage, but someone else said he jumped off a building."

I just stared at them. I couldn't believe that they were sitting around talking about Trevor like that. Like it was nothing. Like he got detention for skipping school or whatever. Then I realized that of course people were talking about him.

Worse than that… I would have been talking about him too if it wasn't my brother. I felt sick, and didn't know what to say.

Ryan saw that I was getting upset, and he freaked out. He yelled, "Can't you see he doesn't want to talk about it, you asshat? Mind your own business!"

They were like, "Geez, dude… Chill out. Whatever, man." And they wandered away.

I lost my appetite, so I shoved my lunch away and started walking to Mr. B's office. By the time I got to the hallway, Ryan, Tasha and Keziah were beside me. I stopped and sat down against the wall, and they sat too.

Keziah said, "He really was an asshat. You'd have to have your head wedged firmly up your ass to say something so stupid."

I laughed, because I'd never really thought about what "asshat" meant. I just thought it was a funny insult, but now that I pictured it, it was hilarious. I thanked Ryan for telling them off, and even though it was cheesy, I told them thanks for walking out with me. Tasha asked if I needed to see Mr. Blackwell, and I said that was where I had been headed, but now I really just wanted to sit with them for a bit. Keziah said if I wanted to talk about it, they would listen. So, I did. I told them how much I hated it when people said "committed suicide," because it sounds like a crime or something. I said that it bothered me that they were gossiping about Trevor, and that I hated that he would be remembered as the kid that jumped off the warehouse. They all said that wasn't true. That people wouldn't do that. But I told them I know it's true, because there was a kid in my third grade class who got hit by a car while he was riding his bike, and he died, and now I can't even remember his name or what he looked like, but I remember he's the kid who died riding his bike. He's the one who everyone's parents remind them of as a warning. "You need to wear a helmet, and be careful crossing the street with your bike. Remember that boy in third grade."

They got quiet, because they knew exactly who I was talking about, and that's all they could remember about him too.

It's so messed up.

20

Today Mom, Dad and I drove over and picked up Tasha so we could go to the warehouse. Her mom was really nice. She hugged my mom and told her how sorry she was to hear about Trevor, then she said that Tasha had told her a lot about me, and Tasha's face turned all red. Then Mom told her not to be embarrassed, because I pretty much talked about *her* constantly. We rolled our eyes at each other, but my face felt super-hot, so I knew I was as red as she was. Then her mom said she had bought some cat food and treats for us to take to the warehouse. Mom had bought a big bag too, so we would have plenty of food to feed them regularly for a long time.

When we got there, we all got out of the car, and Mom looked up at the roof and started crying. Dad walked over and he just stood there with her, hugging her while Tasha and I got the food out of the trunk. We had three small cans of wet food for the kittens, and a bag of the crunchy stuff for the big ones. We popped open the first can, and almost immediately the striped kitten came running through a hole in the bottom of the fence.

Tasha laughed and said, "That must be Kevin!"

It was pretty funny. As we opened the other cans, Wilbern and Berniece came up, too, but they were a little more shy. I was surprised by how much they had grown since the last time I saw them. They didn't look too skinny, so I figured someone else was feeding them too. We put the cans down and backed away to give them space. Kevin was the first one to start, of course, and he made growly sounds while he was eating like he was afraid someone was going to take his food.

Mom and Dad came and sat on the ground with us to watch them eat. Kevin wolfed his can like it was a pie eating contest, then he ran over and shoved Berniece away from hers. Mom walked over, picked up the can and said, "Come here, baby girl," and she put the can down a couple of feet away. Berniece was licking her chops and cleaning her face, and she stopped and did a slow blink, then slowly walked over to the can. She started eating out of it, and when Kevin came over to try again, Mom moved to get up, but Berniece hissed and punched him in the face, and he took off.

Tasha said I should have tried that with human Kevin when he stole my Doritos.

As we sat there, some of the adult cats peeked out, then they slowly came over to the dry food that we scattered on the ground. They would jump any time we moved quickly or talked too loudly, so we just sat and watched them eat for a while, just like I used to do with Trev. I knew he would have wanted me to keep coming out here to feed them. It made me feel good, but it also made me miss him like crazy.

For once, I was okay with the quiet because if I had tried to talk, I would have cried.

21

Today Mom was talking about getting what she called
an "urn necklace." I asked her what that meant, and she told me
they make jewelry that holds ashes. She's looking at one that's
just a little silver tube kind of thing that opens up, and you put
a little bit of ashes in it.

I must have looked like I felt, because she said, "What's
wrong? Do you think it's morbid?"

I asked her what "morbid" meant, and she said it
basically means creepy or weird. I felt bad, but I did think it
was a little bit creepy. I didn't know that people did that. She
said that having his ashes at home made her feel a little better,
and she wanted to be able to take a little of him everywhere
with her. She also said that she understood how I felt because

before we lost Trev, she would have thought it was creepy, too, but now it's just part of her life.

"I'm sorry," she said. "It comforts me, and I'm desperate for comfort."

It's like death doesn't feel real when it's someone you don't know. You hear about it, and you can feel bad about it, but it's a totally different thing when it's someone you love and see every day. Last year there was a kid in my class whose dad had cancer, and he died. I remember thinking that I couldn't imagine what it would be like to lose someone in my family. Like, I couldn't even picture it because it made me feel bad, so I would stop thinking about it. Now that it's happened, I can't stop thinking about it, and I realize it's a thousand times worse than I could ever have imagined. Mom was right. It really is like a nightmare you can't wake up from.

I looked up the word "morbid" and one of the definitions was, "Morbid is the word used to describe anyone who spends too much time thinking about death or disease."

I went back downstairs to talk to Mom because I felt bad about telling her the jewelry idea was weird.

I said, "I guess we're all morbid now, Mom, because Trevor's death is pretty much all we think about."

She said, "Is it still considered morbid when it's part of your life? I don't think we're obsessed with it, I just think we're trying to process it."

I said that it seemed like it would have been easier if he had been sick with cancer, or had an accident or something, and she said, "Depression *is* like cancer. Cancer starts out small, then it crowds out the healthy tissue in your body. Depression also starts out small, then it grows inside your head. It takes over, and crowds out the good stuff. It crowds out the joy. It crowds out the hope."

I said I wished he would have told us how he was really feeling. I wished he would have given us a chance to help him somehow.

Mom said, "We did know. We knew he was depressed. We tried to help him with medication and therapy, and we thought he would get better. We thought that suicide was something that only happened to other people."

Boy, were we wrong.

22

At school today, Mrs. Corte told me how much better my paper was, and I told her that Tasha had helped me work on it. She said she loved the idea of having another student help me while I was struggling and asked if it would be okay if she asked Tasha to continue helping me for a while.

I tried to be all chill and said I thought that would be okay, but inside I was doing backflips. I get to spend more time with Tasha without looking desperate and having to ask with the risk of getting turned down? Ummm... Yes, please!

She brought Tasha up to her desk and asked if she would have time to work with me some because my work had improved so much with her help.

Tasha said, "Of course! I'm happy to help Cody!" Then she looked at me and smiled.

We sat down, and I told her I knew she was busy with the play, and that I understood if she didn't have time, but she said she wanted to help me. Then she asked if I would help her work on memorizing her lines. She said all I had to do was read the other parts that came before her lines. I felt a little weird about it, but since it was just in front of her, and not in front of an audience, I figured it would be okay. Also, it made me feel better to be doing something to help her too.

I told Mom about it when I got home, and she said it sounded like a great idea, and that she really liked Tasha. She said she'd call her mom to figure out when we would get started. I figured it would happen in a couple of days or so, but the next thing I knew, she was on her way over, and she brought her bike so we could take a ride after we finished working on homework and lines for her play.

We got the boring class stuff out of the way, and seriously, she really helped me a lot. She's super smart, but she's not like, "I'm better than you" about it. I told her I usually do okay in school, but I've just been really distracted, and can't concentrate. I don't want her to think I'm a total doofus.

She just smiled and said, "Stop! I know that already! It's okay."

Then it was time to work on her lines for the play. We were reading the part where Jafar is talking to Iago. I wasn't sure if I should try to read it normal, or if she wanted me to do it like Jafar in the movie, so I asked.

She said, "You mean do I want you to do it in character?"

"Ummm... yeah. I guess that's what I mean," I said.

"Would you mind trying it? It will help me remember my part."

Crap. Why did I ask? I got all freaked out all of the sudden, like I was performing or whatever, but I tried. It helped that she was so good at doing her part. She completely changed her voice, and the way she was standing and everything. I started laughing, and she turned red.

She goes, "Am I doing it wrong?"

I said, "Oh my god! Are you *kidding*? You're hilarious!" It was actually way more fun than I thought it was going to be, and I started getting into it.

When we finished, she goes, "You're really good at this, Cody! You should audition for something!"

It was cool to hear that, but I would never be able to do it. The thought of it terrifies me.

We decided to ride our bikes to the warehouse to feed the cats. Mom said it was okay since we still had plenty of light.

I put cat food in my backpack, and we rode over. I shook the bag, and of course, Kevin came running. We put down the food and backed away from it, and slowly all of the other cats came out to eat.

"There are so many," she said.

There are. It's really sad that they don't have homes, but they all look pretty healthy, and I know we're not the only ones feeding them.

It got quiet as we watched them, and she asked me if it was hard for me to come here. I didn't know how to answer that. I mean, of course it's hard, because I can't help but picture Trev climbing and then jumping. That's the hard part. I can see it in my mind even though I wasn't there when he did it. I always wonder- was he sad or scared or relieved? Did he suffer? Did he regret it as soon as he was in the air? All of those thoughts are awful. But at the same time, it was the last place that he was alive. He was alive at the hospital, but he wasn't conscious. There's something about being here that made me feel a little closer to him too.

I found myself telling her everything I was thinking. It all just came out. I even told her that I thought about climbing up there to put some of his ashes on the roof, and that I wanted to stand up there and see the last thing he saw. I asked her not to tell Mom that I said that, and it didn't matter anyway, because not only was I afraid of doing a play, but I was also afraid of heights.

I kind of laughed and said, "What a wuss, huh? I'm afraid of everything." Then I started crying. I looked over at her, and she was crying too.

She said it was okay to be afraid of things, and that she was afraid of a lot of stuff too. Then she scooted over closer to me, and she put her head on my shoulder, and I did the most terrifying thing of all.

I reached out and held her hand.

We sat there until my hand got all sweaty, and I was trying to decide if I should apologize for my sweaty hand, when she said, "Sorry my hand is all sweaty."

I said, "I was just getting ready to say that."

And she pulled her hand away and goes, "You were getting ready to tell me that my hand is all sweaty?!"

"No! No way! I was going to say *mine* was all sweaty!"

Then we both started laughing, which caused all of the cats to jump and go running back though the hole in the fence to their hiding places, and we laughed again, and held sweaty hands until it was time to go home.

23

Last night I went to bed feeling the best I have felt in a long time. I could still feel Tasha's hand in mine, and the weight of her head on my shoulder, and when I thought about it, my stomach would do a little flip. I went to sleep thinking about myself for a change. Unfortunately, my sleep self wasn't about to let that happen. I dreamed that Trev and I were in this huge old house. It was creeping me out, and I wanted to leave, but he wanted to stay and explore. The next thing I knew, I couldn't find him, so I started running from room to room looking for him. I ended up finding a door to get out of the house, and I went outside, then I heard Trev yelling for me, so I tried to get back in to him, but the door was locked. He was yelling my name over and over, and I kept running around trying to get to him, but I couldn't. When I looked up, he was on the roof looking down at me. I woke up freaked out, and couldn't go back to sleep.

When I got to school, I went straight to Mr. Blackwell's office. I told him that I had something really cool that happened, then I had a nightmare, and I woke up mad. I'm pissed. I'm pissed because my big brother should be here so I could tell him that I held hands with a girl, and he would tell me how great it was, and he would tell me about the first girl he held hands with, and he would say, "Did your hand get all sweaty?" And I would go, "Oh my god, YES!!" And then we would laugh. Then I could ask him if it was weird for him when he saw her at school. I could ask him what to do, and how to act with her in front of other people, because I don't know how to do this. I mean, do I, like, sit next to her at lunch now instead of across from her? I'm pissed because I was so happy, and I felt so good, then I dreamed I failed him again. I mean, it doesn't take some kind of dream explainer or whatever to tell me that my brain doesn't want me to forget to feel bad. Like, I shouldn't forget that I wasn't there for him. I shouldn't forget that he chose to die. I shouldn't forget that

Mom is getting skinnier, and sometimes she looks like she just

woke up when I get home from school, and Dad leaves for

work before I leave for school, and isn't coming home until

late at night, so sometimes I go days without even seeing him.

Everything has changed. *Everything*. Our lives are completely

different, and it's his fault. He made a choice that screwed up

everyone else's lives, and I am *pissed off*. I feel like I don't

deserve to have anything good happen to me anymore.

I dumped it all out there, and by the end, I was doing

that toddler cry thing where their breath comes in and goes out

with a shudder, and it happens every other word or so. Mr. B.

just sat there and let me freak out, then when I finally calmed

down, I said, "I'm sorry. You must think I'm a douche... I

mean... a real jerk for being mad at someone who was sick."

He shook his head, and he said, "Nope. Not in the least.

I think you are completely justified in your feelings. All of

them. It sucks, Cody. It's not fair. It would be strange if you

didn't feel angry. I would be pissed if I were you too. You're not a douche. You are a normal kid who is trying to deal with a horrible situation."

I just nodded my head and waited while he wrote a note explaining why I was tardy. I was still pretty sure that I was totally douchey. I turned around to leave, and he goes, "And Cody, just try telling Tasha the truth. Just tell her how you feel. She's probably wondering about the same things you're worried about."

I was already sitting down when Tasha came into the cafeteria. She looked a little like she was trying to figure out where to sit, and then Keziah sat down, so she just sat in her normal spot. At the end of lunch, she asked me if I would go to the drama room with her after school to check her rehearsal schedule, so after our last class we walked there together, and we were able to talk. I told her that I really wanted to sit with her at lunch, but I didn't want to make things weird. She said she felt the same way, and that maybe we could sit together and stuff, but save holding hands and other stuff for when we were away from school. She said something else too, but I didn't hear all of it, because my brain froze when she said

"other stuff". I'm not real sure what she means by that, but I'm

super excited to find out.

Holy crap.

24

I sat next to Tasha at lunch today, then Keziah came in and sat next to her, so Ryan just sat on the other side of the table looking like he didn't know what to do. It was super awkward until Keziah got up and walked around and sat next to him, which didn't help very much, because then he looked scared because a girl was sitting next to him. It got better when she handed him a chocolate covered peanut butter Oreo. That's pretty much all it takes to make Ryan happy. It's like giving a dog a treat. When Tasha saw what happened, she nudged me with her knee under the table, then she just left her leg there. Her thigh was right up against my thigh. My face got all hot, and I couldn't think clearly. I only ended up eating about half of my sandwich. When it was time to go, and she moved, my leg felt cold where hers had been, and I wished we could have stayed there longer.

When I got home, Mom wasn't downstairs. I wasn't sure if she was home, so I went out and looked in the garage, and her car was there. I went upstairs to her room, but she wasn't there. It scared me. I walked over to Trev's room, and she was asleep on his bed. I woke her up, and she was startled, and said, "What are you doing home already? Is everything okay?" When I told her school was over, she apologized and told me she had taken a nap, and must have slept longer than she thought. I told her she was still in the pajamas that she was wearing when I left for school this morning, and I asked her when she laid down for her nap. She put her hand over her mouth and started to cry, and she said that she went back to bed after I left for school, and just slept off and on all day. I hugged her while she cried for what felt like forever, then I told her to go take a shower, and come downstairs.

I heated up some tomato soup, and made a grilled cheese sandwich, and cut it into four long pieces, because she liked to dip it in the soup to eat it. When she came into the kitchen, she thanked me and said she was sorry for worrying me, and that she was a terrible mother. It felt super weird to be taking care of my mom who has always taken care of me. I really didn't know what to say, but I knew I had to tell her she was wrong, so I said, "You're the best mom I know. You're just really sad right now, and I don't blame you for that. It would be weird if you weren't sad, Mom. This just sucks."

Mom just looked at me, and she had the saddest smile I've ever seen, and she said, "Yes. It *does* suck, doesn't it? It sucks big time. It sucks… it sucks… ass."

I just sat there with my mouth open. I mean, she's right, but I've never heard my mom say ass, or any other bad word for that matter. I said, "I can't believe you just said 'ass!'"

Then she picked up a piece of grilled cheese, and she dunked it in her soup and took a bite. She closed her eyes, and with her mouth all full, she told me that it tasted better than anything she had tried to eat in weeks. Then she looked at me, and told me to watch my language. Then she smiled.

Since I didn't eat much of my lunch, I had made myself one too, and we sat together and ate and talked about how we were ruining our dinner, but we didn't care. She ate almost the whole sandwich, then she pulled out a word search puzzle book, and I did my homework.

It was such a small, normal thing, but it was cool, you know? It felt good.

When I came up to my room to journal before bed, I had two texts. One was from Ryan, and the other from Tasha. They both said the same thing. "Pizza day tomorrow!" Except Ryan's was all caps. Dude loves him some pizza.

Tasha sent a second text that said, "Do you still bring dessert on pizza day?"

I sent one back that said, "We haven't done that before, but I have no idea why, because it's freaking brilliant!"

Then I sent one to Ryan telling him to bring dessert anyway, and he replied, "OMG... Why haven't we done that before?!?!"

I was still laughing when I got a reply from Tasha with a laughing emoji and a heart. I sat here on my bed smiling like an idiot.

She's really cool.

25

I came home today with no homework, so I asked Mom

if I could ride my bike over to feed the cats. I thought she was

going to say no, but she said it was okay. I grabbed some cat

food and treats and put them in my backpack and headed over.

It's weird. When I get close enough where I can see the

building in the distance, my stomach sinks. I know it

sounds weird because it's not like I don't think he died, but

sometimes I think about what I would have done or said to him

if I had ridden up and seen him on the roof. In my mind, I

always climb up to him, and I am able to talk him down.

I got off my bike and got the food out and shook the

bag. Kevin came around the corner like a fat, furry rocket.

Then one by one the rest of them came creeping out, except for

Wilbern and Berniece. They always come out together. I

poured the food out in a line, and stepped back a bit and sat on the ground to watch them eat.

I was just quiet for a while, and then I pulled out the treats and rattled the bag. They all jumped a little and looked up at me. Most of them went back to eating, but Kevin was super curious about what I was doing. I put some treats in my hand and held it out in front of me. He slowly started walking toward me, and every few steps, he would stop and give me a slow blink, then he'd move toward me again. He got, like, just a couple of feet away and was trying to smell what was in my hand, so I put the back of my hand on the ground and held my breath. He wanted to take it, but I could tell he was scared so I turned my hand over and dumped the treats in front of me. Poor guy was too scared to come over and eat it. I felt bad for him. I know what it's like to be too afraid to do what I want to do. What I *need* to do sometimes.

For some strange reason I can't explain, I walked over to the fence in front of the building and put my fingers in the chain link. I looked around to make sure no one was watching, but there wasn't anyone around, so I put my hands up higher and put the toes of my shoes in there, too. I was clinging to the fence with my heart pounding like crazy, and I started climbing. I got all the way up to where the barbed wire started, and I just hung on there for a while. I looked over, and Kevin was staring at me, so, like, if it's not crazy enough to be clinging to a fence, I said, "It's okay, Kevin." I don't know if he understood me or just got bored watching me hang there, but he turned and left, then I climbed back down to the ground.

It was a start.

26

We've got Tasha's play coming up soon, and Mom said
I needed to wear something nicer than jeans or sweats. I went
to check, and my one pair of dress pants and shirt fit okay, but
my good shoes hurt my feet, so we had to go shopping. Dad
came home early enough to go shopping with us. The first
place we went to was Ross. My family loves to shop for
bargains. When Trev was still alive, we would go to thrift
stores and try on weird clothes and stuff. We have tons of pics
of me and Trev in stuff like tutus, Viking helmets, and animal
print jackets. This one time, Trev bought a pink princess
toddler bike, and he rode that thing everywhere. He looked like
a big circus bear riding it. His knees came up to his ears when
he pedaled. He also bought a unicycle once, and he practiced
for weeks. He fell over and over again until one day it finally

clicked, and he was riding it. He saw a video of a guy riding a unicycle and playing bagpipes that blew out fire, and he said that was his goal in life. He kept an eye out for bagpipes at the thrift store, but he never found any.

Anyway, while we were back in the shoe department, I looked over at Dad, and he was just standing there, staring at something. I walked over, and it was a pair of huge shoes. He had tears streaming down his face, and when he realized I was there, he looked at me, and said, "I'm sorry", then he walked out of the store.

I don't know why, but our Ross always has really big shoes. Like, a size 15. *Huge.* Trev would always find the biggest pair of shoes they had, and he would put them on and stand there with his hands on his hips, his chest out, and his chin tilted up, like he was some kind of superhero or something, and he would wait for one of us to walk up and see him. He didn't even care if strangers in the store saw him. It always made us laugh. I knew exactly why Dad was upset. I could picture Trev there, too, and I got a big lump in my throat.

I went to find Mom and tell her that Dad left the store, so we went out and found him in the car. He apologized for running out, and for crying like that.

He said, "I know that I haven't been around like I need to. I just… he's everywhere except work. That's the only place that I don't have any memories of him. The only place that I don't picture him, because he was never there. I can't even go to the store…"

Mom said, "I never want to leave the house, because I want to be where all of the memories are. All of his things. It comforts me. But I know everyone grieves in their own way. There's no right or wrong way to do it. We just have to take it moment by moment, until we work our way up to hour by hour, then day by day."

Dad leaned over and let Mom put her arms around him for a bit, then we all got out of the car and went back inside to try again.

27

Tasha has been super busy with final rehearsals for the show, but she still sends me texts, and she sent a pic of herself in her costume. She had been afraid that she would be in a big, puffy, feathery thing with a huge beak, like the ones you see the sign swingers wear. There's a sandwich shop in town that has a dude outside dressed like a giant pickle with a chef's hat on. Even with the big costume on, you can tell he seems ashamed. He never swings the sign. He just slouches there, holding the sign down in front of his thighs. He's just a big old sad pickle. You gotta feel for the guy, you know? Anyway, Tasha's costume wasn't like that at all. It was a red dress with red tights and yellow shoes. She wore a headband with some feathers in it, and the back of the dress had bright colored layers of cloth on the skirt part that were like her tail feathers.

She texted, "What do you think?"

I sent back, "I think you look beautiful!" and I sent it before I could change my mind. It's the truth. Here she was, dressed like a freaking parrot, but she still managed to look really pretty. To be honest, I was worried that she would be embarrassed to wear her costume, so I was really relieved for her.

My phone dinged, and she had sent, "You are the sweetest!"

I was gonna send a heart, but I looked and was pumped to find out that they had a red parrot emoji, so I sent that instead. That's when I realized what I was going to get for her.

I went on Amazon and found a stuffed Iago, then I went to ask Mom if we could order it, and I would pay her back. She agreed, and she said that for opening night you're supposed to give flowers. I hadn't ever been to a play, so I didn't know how it worked. She said she would take me to get them the day of the play. I showed her the picture that Tasha sent, and she said, "Aaaaaaaawwww…" and put her hand on her chest, and said, "She is adorable! You really like her, huh?"

I said I did, and even though it was weird to talk to Mom about girl stuff, I told her that Tasha's been really cool about listening to me talk about Trev and stuff, and that I could tell her things I couldn't tell anyone else. That at first, I was super nervous with her, but now it feels more comfortable, and I would want to be her friend even if I didn't have a crush on her. I even told her that I held her hand at the warehouse. Mom's eyes started watering, but she was smiling. She said she was glad I had something so nice happening when things have been so hard. I told her that sometimes I feel bad for being excited, and for feeling happy. She just nodded her head, and said she knew exactly what I was talking about.

She said, "I think, 'What kind of mother am I if I can laugh when I've failed my son so badly?'" I started to tell her that she didn't fail anything, but she stopped me, and said, "I decided before I had children that I wanted to be a stay at home mom. Making sure I am always here for you and Trevor has been the most important thing in this world to me, and now he's gone. I couldn't help him. I wasn't enough. No matter how many times I tell myself that he was ill... that it was beyond my control... that I did everything in my power to keep him with us... I still feel like I failed."

I didn't know what to say, because I feel like I failed him too. I didn't know how to make her feel better when I felt the same way, and I knew that nothing anyone said would make me feel any different, so it wouldn't help her either.

So, I just sat there until she left the room, and I could hear her sniffling in the hallway. I've gotten very used to that sound.

28

I was really missing Trev today, so I went into his

room. I laid on his bed, and Mom still hadn't cleaned or

changed his sheets or anything, so it still smelled like him. I

just laid there with my eyes closed, and pictured him the way

he used to be. I read that the sense of smell can trigger

memories more than any other sense, and I believe it.

He was always pretty messy. Mom used to get onto him

for having trash in his room, like food wrappers and stuff, and I

saw a Yoo-Hoo bottle on the floor next to his hamper. It was

one of his favorite drinks. He would pretend he was wine

tasting when he would drink one at dinner. He would hold the

bottle and swirl it around, and talk about how you had to aerate

it, then he would put his nose over the opening and take a big

sniff, then he would take a sip and hold it in his mouth and swish it around and gargle it, then he would say something like, "It has a delightfully forward chocolate taste, with a creamy mouth feel, and leaves an aftertaste of high fructose corn syrup. This 2018 Yoo-Hoo would pair nicely with a grilled salmon filet, or a Tyson chicken tender." He was the best. So funny, and so smart. It sucks that all I have now are memories. I'll never have a new Trev story.

I started digging around in his backpack, and I found a sketch pad. He was always doodling stuff. He was an amazing artist. As I flipped through it, I could see that his drawings went from animals and trees and stuff to people. The drawings got... I don't know, like, *darker*, I guess, as I turned the pages. There was a picture of a man's head, and his face looked like he was, like, suffering or something. The top of his head was open, and there were spiders, snakes and bugs crawling out of it. There was another drawing of a man with his mouth wide open, and a hand growing out of his head, like it was reaching for something. They were so sad. It made me realize how much pain he was feeling. How sick he was. On the last page, there was a drawing of a man pushing a huge rock up a steep hill.

There was something familiar about it, so I googled, "man pushing rock up a hill," and learned that it was a guy named Sisyphus from Greek mythology. He was punished by the gods, because he thought he was smarter than Zeus. His punishment was to push this huge rock up the hill every day, and at the end of each day, it would roll back down, and he would have to push it back up for all eternity. I guess that's how Trev felt. He would make it through another day lugging around his sadness, and the next day, there it was again until he couldn't do it anymore. He climbed and climbed every day, until finally, instead of reaching the top and climbing back down to do it again, he reached the top, and jumped. He just couldn't carry it any more.

This was the first time I have been able to imagine how he must have felt. They say that a picture is worth a thousand words, and now I understand what that really means. These drawings told me his story more than any note he could have left. Seeing his pain in his artwork made it real. I wouldn't want to live like that either.

I don't think he was trying to get away from us. He was trying to get away from himself.

29

I heard a knock at the door, so I went to answer it, and it was a lady who lives in our neighborhood. We aren't, like, friends or anything, so I don't even know her name. She asked for Mom, so I turned to yell for her but remembered that she hates it when I yell for her, especially in front of company, so I invited the lady in and went to get her. The lady brought a pan of food over for us, and Mom thanked her and had me take it into the kitchen. I stayed in the kitchen for a bit, because I wanted to see what it was. I was concentrating on pulling back the foil quietly, without ripping it, when I heard Mom sounding upset. I went to eavesdrop, and I heard the lady say, "I'm sorry! I was just trying to say something comforting!"

Mom replied, "It's not comforting for you to say that you understand how I feel because your son moved away, and you miss him. You have no idea how I feel! Your son did not jump off of a warehouse! You didn't sit in a hospital waiting room for five hours waiting to find out if you were going to bring him home, or decide what to do with his body! Your son's remains are not in a box on your coffee table! It's not even close to the same thing!"

The lady was crying, and she kept apologizing, but Mom was freaking out. She turned and yelled for me to bring the food back to her, so I put the foil back down, ran out, and tried to hand the lady back her food. She told me we could keep it, so I looked up at Mom, and she took it out of my hands, and shoved it over to her. The lady took it, and ran out the door.

Mom walked over and sat down on the sofa with her head in her hands. I sat down beside her, and rubbed her back. She told me she was sorry, and I said, "For what? That was a stupid thing for her to say. I had a kid at school who told me that he knew how I felt, because his dog died. His *dog*. I just mumbled, 'thanks,' and walked away. I wish I had let him have it like you did, Mom. I was thinking all of the same things, but I didn't have the guts to unleash on him like you did on her."

She actually laughed, and said, "I *did* unleash. It felt really good."

I asked Mom what the lady's name was, and Mom started laughing even harder and said she had no idea. She lived down the street, and drove a Volvo, so Mom always thought of her as Volvo Lady. I told her that she did the right thing by sending home the food. I'd peeked at it, and it was tuna with noodles and canned peas. Super gross. By that time, we were both laughing.

People are weird. I don't know why they can't just say they're sorry. Or even that they don't know what to say. Because what *do* you say? Don't even think that you can understand it if you haven't had it happen to you, you know? Just say you're sorry, and be grateful that you *don't* know how we feel.

I'm just glad she didn't bring a lasagna. I wouldn't have wanted to give that back.

30

We have a teacher named Mrs. Starks. She's a great teacher, but she spits a little when she talks. Every once in a while, when you walk into her class and sit down, she will yell, "Upset the apple cart!" This means that everyone gets up and runs to a different seat in the classroom for their new seat assignment. Since the front row is in the splash zone, everyone runs for the back of the room. I got a sweet spot in the back row at the beginning of the year because Trev had warned me about her, so when it's time, I just jump up and do a quick circle around my desk and sit back down. Today at lunch, Keziah walked in looking upset, and when Tasha asked her what was wrong, she yelled, "Up-thet the apple cart!" just like Sylvester the cat from the Bugs Bunny cartoons. Ryan was mid-drink, and he got choked and blew water out of his nose.

Of course, we were all dying laughing, when Ms. Parker, one of my old teachers that I never really liked, walked up and said, "I was just coming over to tell you I was sorry to hear about your brother, and see how you were holding up, but it looks like you're doing quite well." And she walked away.

Kind of ruined the moment.

It seems like everything that happens has Trev's death hanging over it. It's always there. Sometimes in the back of my mind, but most of the time it's in the front row. The splash-zone. I can't help but feel... I don't know, I guess I can't help but feel judged, you know? Like, no matter what I do, it's wrong. If I mope around and cry a lot, I'm not "getting better," but if I laugh with my friends, I feel like people will think I'm not sad enough. That I'm "getting better" too quickly. I can't just *be* anymore. I can't just feel what I feel without wondering if it's okay to feel it. And it's not like I can control it, because it's feelings. I mean, I spend a lot of time pretending everything is okay or whatever, but the feelings are just *there*. I can't change those. And no matter what those feelings are, I'm afraid to show them in front of people.

It changed everyone else's mood at the table too. It got quiet, and more than a little bit awkward, and we all just sat around eating, and listening to Ryan sniff as his nose dripped water.

When I got home from school, Mom was trying to put some of Trev's ashes in her new necklace. I could tell she was having trouble because her hands were shaking, so I offered to help her. The thing that holds the ashes looks like a bullet, but it's silver with abalone shell in it. I was surprised at how beautiful it was. I told Mom that, and she smiled her sad smile, and said, "It really is, isn't it?" I unscrewed the top, and put in the tiny funnel that came with it, scooped a little into the tiny urn, and screwed the lid back on. As I did, I just started thinking about how much things had changed in the last few months, from the time Trev came back home until now. If you would have told me six months ago that I would be sitting at the table helping my mom put my brother's ashes in a necklace, I would have said you were crazy.

Since Mom told me about the necklace, I've been thinking about taking some ashes for myself. Like, I want to keep some in my room, which of course, was Trev's room. I feel like he belongs there. I've also been thinking of taking some to the warehouse to leave them there if I work up the guts to climb to the roof. I mean, when... when I work up the guts. I know he loved it there, and it was the last place he was alive. I asked Mom if I could have some for my room. I didn't mention the warehouse. She said it would be fine, and asked if I wanted to get a small urn or something to put them in. I told her that if it was okay with her, I would like to just put them in a small baggie, and keep them in one of his chalk bags from his climbing gear. Mom closed her eyes, and I saw tears start to squeeze out, and she said that she thought it was a lovely idea.

So here I sit, holding my brother's ashes in my hand. I can't believe this is my life.

31

I haven't recorded myself in a few days. I skip a couple

of days here and there sometimes because nothing new is really

happening, or because I'm just not feeling it, you know? Mr. B

says those are the days when I need it the most. I'm sure he's

right, but sometimes I just… can't. The past couple of days

have been bad. I don't know exactly how to explain it but, like,

you know those videos where there's a ton of people walking

down a sidewalk, and they're in fast forward motion, but

there's one person in the middle of all of it who's just standing

there looking lost? That's me. That's how I feel. It's like I'm

just … stuck, but everyone else is running around, like, *living*.

It feels wrong to keep going. It feels like we're leaving him

behind.

I think about how I wish I could have been there to save

him, and I've talked about that, but sometimes it goes even

further. Like at night, when I can't fall asleep, I still think about what it would have been like to bring him home from the hospital. Like, if he had survived the surgery, you know? I picture the surgeon walking into the waiting room, and kneeling down to put her hand on Mom's knee, and saying, "He's going to be okay." I picture moving all of his stuff to the game room downstairs, so he wouldn't have to worry about getting up the stairs. I picture him in a wheelchair, and I can totally see him spinning in circles, and doing wheelies. I picture him with prosthetic legs. The cool ones like the runners use that are metal, that don't look like real feet. He had such good balance that I know he would have been walking in no time. Running, climbing, even. Then the stairs wouldn't be a big deal. I'd move back into my old room, and I would be happy to do it. I wouldn't feel sorry for myself because I was losing the cool room. I'd be happy because he was here. I picture him playing video games with me, and cracking up at those videos where people have big wipeouts. He loved those. We always groaned and doubled over whenever we saw one where someone took a nut shot, then we would laugh. Always. We always laughed.

The other day, one of my mom's friends said, "I can't imagine losing one of my children."

Mom said, "I can't either."

I know that sounds weird or whatever, but that's exactly it. Even though it's our reality, I still can't imagine it. I can't imagine never seeing him again.

Dad always told me not to watch horror movies, but I did it anyway at Ryan's house. His parents didn't want him to either, but we would stay up after they went to bed and watch them with his big brother.

He would say, "Whatever, dudes. But if one of you little wussies wets the bed 'cause you're scared, you'll never live it down. I'll be making fun of you when you visit me in the nursing home."

And I did get scared. Holy crap, I was terrified. I would lay there and think about what would happen if a killer came into the house and killed everyone else, and I was the only one left. I would try to think about what I would do and stuff, but I never figured it out. I would make myself think about something else so that I could calm down and go to sleep. I could convince myself that no matter how scary and awful it was, it wasn't real.

Now I do the same thing, but, like, it *is* real. I tell myself that it can't be. How can it be? How can my brother have died in such a violent and awful way? How?

So it makes me feel better to plan. To imagine him coming home. To think about how I miss him, but that's okay, because he will be home soon.

I lie to myself.

I can't picture my life without him in it, so sometimes I just don't.

32

I haven't been able to hang out with Ryan or Tasha much lately. I see them at school and stuff, but that's it. Tasha is in the middle of "Hell Week" with the play. She explained that that's when they add in all the extra stuff, like the lights and costumes, and it's super complicated, so they have to rehearse every day until the show opens. Ryan has been busy too, because he and Keziah have started dating. I mean, I guess it's not really "dating" because they don't really go out like older kids who have cars and stuff, but they're like me and Tasha. They really like each other, so they hang out as much as they can, and they text all the time and stuff. Part of me feels angry and sad that he isn't really there for me right now, but I guess I did the same thing to him before Tasha was in the play, and if I'm being real honest, I'm going to do it again when the play is over this weekend.

I've been going to feed the cats pretty much every day, and they're still scared of me. When I get too close, or make a sudden movement, any that are exploring outside run to get back behind the fence where they feel safer. I don't really blame them. Their lives are pretty hard, living alone outside. I would imagine some of them used to be pets, but their owners abandoned them for whatever reason. I wouldn't trust people either.

Today when I went to the warehouse, I decided it was time to at least get over the fence. I put my backpack on backwards, with the straps on my back and the bag part in the front, so that it would be between me and the barbed wire. I don't know how Trev did it, but it made me wonder if he did it the same way. Then I started thinking that maybe his backpack was on the roof, and there was a note in it or something. I keep the chalk bag with his ashes in it in my backpack for when I get brave enough to get up there someday.

I climbed up to the barbed wire part of the fence, with the cats all staring up at me from the other side, then I carefully gripped the top two wires, and tried to squeeze them together like I did when I climbed the barbed wire fence at my grandma and grandpa's farm. The wires on this fence weren't as loose as the old farm fence, so I couldn't squeeze them together. I just had to grab the top wire, and pull myself up. I threw my leg over without snagging my pants, and the backpack worked to keep me from getting hurt by the barbs, but I got it snagged, so when I tried to go down the other side, I was sort of hanging there for a minute. I'm glad it was just the cats watching because I know I must have looked like an idiot. Like a turtle on its back. I finally got unhooked and climbed down the other side.

I was a little nervous, because I had only seen the building from outside the fence. I walked over to the building, and studied it up close. It's a really old building, with five balconies. The first one starts on the second floor, so it's six stories tall. The thought of climbing up there seemed very real now, and very terrifying. I decided not to try to climb it today, but getting over the fence felt like a huge accomplishment.

When I turned around, I thought about where Trev must have landed when he jumped. I didn't know where it was exactly, but to think that I had maybe just walked across it gave me chills.

The cats had all scattered to their hiding places by then. All except for Kevin. He was sitting a few feet away from me, staring. I pulled the food out of my backpack, and when the other cats heard it, they started slowly coming out. I pulled out a piece of food and put it on the ground in front of me. Kevin did a slow blink, and he started coming my way. I was holding my breath because I didn't want to scare him. He leaned over and ate the food with his eyes on me the whole time. I pulled another piece of food out, and he jumped and took a couple of steps back. I took out a few pieces and put one on the ground in front of me again, and he came over and took it. Then I put one on my knee and waited. He would look at it, then he would look up at me, and finally, he walked over and took the food. I fed him some more food on my knee. He ate it all, then he did a little head butt into my knee, like he was saying "thank you," and he walked away.

Another accomplishment.

It felt good. It made me feel like I was doing what I was supposed to do. I walked back over and put my hands on the warm bricks, and looked straight up. The climb looked endless. I don't know if I can do this, but I want to do it. I need to do it. I am going to get up to the roof sometime soon. I just know it.

33

Tonight was the opening night of Aladdin. I had the stuffed Iago in a gift bag, and I was going to get red roses, but I read that red roses mean love, and I didn't want to scare her off. I looked it up and, like, each of the different colors of roses means something different. I decided to just skip all of that, and Mom and Dad stopped at the store and helped me pick out a bouquet that's all different colors.

When we got there, as soon as we walked in to sit down, I started getting butterflies in my stomach. I was super nervous for her. I shouldn't have been. She was amazing. I looked over at Mom and Dad at one point when she was doing a scene, and they were both smiling. Like *really* smiling. Mom leaned over and said, "She is fantastic!" I just nodded and smiled back. At intermission, Dad said she was stealing the show.

After it was over, when they were coming out for the curtain call, she came out with Jafar- and Mom and Dad stood up and Dad did a big whistle with his thumb and finger in the corners of his mouth. I stood up with them and saw that her family was standing up for her too. I was clapping and smiling like a big old doofus, and I could see her looking around at the audience, like, trying to smile, but not really smiling because she was looking for something. Then she spotted me. And she smiled a real smile, and gave a little wave, and it was the best feeling in the world.

She had told me at school that Mrs. Araujo won't let the performers go out to see everyone until they are out of their costumes, so I shoved my way through the crowd to the door of the dressing room and waited. One of the other girls came out and asked if I was looking for Tasha, and I said yes, so she told me that I could go in because there were only two girls in there, and they were both dressed. I just stood there feeling weird about going into the dressing room, and she goes, "Go on, Cody. She's waiting for you." I walked in, and she was in there with Jessica, whose Resting Bitch Face became Active Bitch

Face when she saw me with flowers and a gift bag. Tasha ran over and hugged me and was talking about how beautiful the flowers were. She pulled open the gift bag, pulled out the stuffed bird, and she hugged me again.

Jessica goes, "So, what is he? Your boyfriend?"

I froze and looked down at the floor because I didn't want to see Tasha be embarrassed, and we hadn't, like, discussed whether or not we were boyfriend and girlfriend. I wanted it to be that way, but we hadn't said the words out loud.

Tasha said, "Yes. He's my boyfriend." Jessica laughed, like she was making fun of her, and Tasha goes, "Don't worry. One of these days a boy will like you enough to give you flowers, too. In the meantime, the ones you got from your mom are really pretty!"

Jessica pretty much ran out of the dressing room, and I lost it. I was just laughing hysterically. When I calmed down, she said, "I hope it's okay that I said you were my boyfriend." Then she started to say how she said it to get to Jessica, but that if I was uncomfortable with it, we didn't have to say that, but I stopped her, and told her that was more than okay. That I wanted her to be my girlfriend. She smiled and thanked me again for the flowers, and the Iago, and then she put them down, put her hands on my shoulders, and pulled me in and kissed me. It happened so fast and so unexpectedly that I didn't have time to worry about whether I was doing it right or not. I thought seeing her looking for me in the audience was the best feeling in the world, but holy crap, this feeling beat it by a mile.

34

After I finished recording earlier, I was still wide awake, so I decided to go hang out in Trev's room. I just wanted to be with his stuff, I guess. I mean, if he was here, I would have told him about the kiss. I was nosing around in his stuff, and I found a post-it-note under an empty Cheetos bag that had "MrVevo_8675309" written on it in his handwriting. When we were little, we had a friend named Noah who had trouble saying our names. He called me "Dewey," and he called Trevor "Vevo," and for some reason, the name "Vevo" just kind of stuck as a nickname. We eventually stopped calling him that, but when he played video games, he still used the name "Mr. Vevo." The number is from an old song that he heard. The guy in the song was singing this girl's phone number over and over again. He was pretty much stalking her, and talking about how she didn't know him, but he knew he could make her happy. Super weird. Like, restraining order weird. Trev made me listen to it, because he thought it was hilarious. It looked like it might be his password for his laptop. Dad had been trying to get into it, but he didn't have any luck. It was still sitting on his desk, plugged in, so I opened it up and turned it on. It remembered his username, so all I had to do was type what was on the post-it-note into the password box.

It worked.

I thought about going to tell Mom and Dad, but they were sleeping, and also, I was crazy curious about what I might find, and wanted plenty of time to look at it alone, which I wouldn't have once they woke up. A part of me wondered if maybe this is where he left a note, and then I could get some answers. I know if he killed himself because of me, and it said so somewhere here, Mom and Dad would never tell me.

The first thing that popped up was a Facebook page with the name "Vevo." Trev always thought Facebook was for old people to show pictures of their kids and grandkids, argue about politics or religion, and show their friends what they were eating for dinner. When I looked closer, I saw that his page only had one friend. It was some girl named Fallon. His profile said that he was 118 years old. His profile picture was a picture of Ed from Ed, Edd and Eddy. Then I saw that he had a message on Facebook Messenger, so I clicked on it. It was from someone named Fallon, and it said, "Haven't heard from you in a while, Vevo. Hope you're okay." I scrolled up through the messages, and started reading from the top. They met while playing Overwatch online. They started out talking about the game, then it moved into more personal stuff. Nothing like, sexual or anything. It was just how they felt about school and friends and stuff like that. Then they started talking about how they both struggled with feeling alone and depressed. He told her he was unhappy, and that he had tried to kill himself while he was away at college, by putting a hose from the exhaust pipe into his car window, but it just made him sick. He said, "I couldn't even do that right." He said that if you looked at his life from the outside, he had everything, but on the inside he felt empty. He couldn't find anything to fill the emptiness.

As I was reading, I realized that she didn't even know his real name, his age, or where he lived. She didn't know anything about him... but she knew *everything* about him. He told her so much. They talked for hours and hours. I couldn't believe it. Here it was. All of it.

And there was nothing at all about me. He didn't even mention that he had a brother. I was partly relieved, but I was also sad and a little mad, to be honest. I mean, I'm glad it wasn't my fault, but, like, at the same time... I don't know... It just feels like maybe I didn't mean much to him at all, you know?

He only mentioned Mom and Dad once, and he said that they had always limited his video gaming time when he was at home, but they didn't have any trouble binge watching Game of Thrones for hours on end. It made me laugh a little, because he and I had complained about it when he was still in high school, but we did it in a joking way. He wasn't, like, seriously mad or anything.

I finally went to my bedroom and slept for a while until Mom and Dad got up. I told them immediately that I had gotten into Trev's computer. Dad ran for Trev's room, and yelled

down the hall, asking me how to get in. I showed him, and he

spent hours going through it. Mom would wander in once in a

while and check and see what he was reading, but she couldn't

stay in there long. She would only read a little bit, then she

would cover her mouth, and go into her bedroom to cry.

It was a very quiet day.

He finally came out of the room around dinner time,

and told us that he had been chatting with Fallon. He felt like

he needed to let her know that Trevor was dead. She thought

that it was Trev playing a joke on her at first. She said, "This

isn't funny, Vevo." Then, of course, when she realized it was

really Dad, and that he was serious, she was devastated.

I asked him why he thought that Trevor couldn't talk to

us about it. Why did he tell a stranger? Why was he so open

with someone who didn't even know his real name?

Dad said that was really the point. If he told us, we

would have tried to stop him, but Fallon couldn't. He had

already made up his mind, and there wasn't a thing she could

do to stop him.

35

Today was Sunday, so Tasha got to come over to help

me with homework. We worked on it some at school

sometimes while she was in the play, so I'm doing okay. I

mean, I'm getting mostly C's, and I'm passing everything. My

teachers are all really nice about it and stuff, but I still just

can't concentrate. I'll be reading, then when I turn the page, I

can't remember what I just read. Same still goes for listening to

lectures in class. It's like a Charlie Brown cartoon when the

teacher is talking. It's all just "wah wah wah wah."

We were talking about the play, and she asked what I

thought of it, of course, so I told her the truth. I said I loved her

performance, and that even my Dad said she stole the show. I

really liked it a lot, and the other characters were good, too.

But since I ran Jafar's lines so much practicing with her, I would catch myself sort of mouthing them along with the actor who played him, and it was weird, but he didn't do it like I would have done it. It was disappointing. She said she thought I was better at it too, and I should audition next time. I laughed, but she was serious. She said to just take a drama class next semester, and see if I like it. I hadn't really thought about that. I think I might actually do it. I mean, a class wouldn't be that big of a deal, right?

After we finished homework, we rode our bikes to the warehouse. We had laid out the food, and were just sitting there watching all of the cats eat, when Tasha gasped and said, "Cody! Look!" and pointed at my arm. I looked down, and there was a butterfly just hanging out there. She told me her grandma said that when a butterfly lands on you, it's like getting a kiss from an angel. I'd never heard that before. I just stared at it, trying to decide if I believed in it or not. Like, could it be Trev saying hello? Do I even believe that kind of stuff exists, or is it something people come up with to make themselves feel better? But then, like, what are the chances of having one land on me, and just hang out there, right there where he tried to end his life, you know? I mean, that's never happened to me before. And like, what does it hurt to believe it? To think that maybe he's trying to tell me that he's glad I keep coming here to remember him? Is that such a bad thing? The more I sat there and stared at it, the more choked up I got. Tasha was cool about it. I know she saw what was happening, and she just sat there with me and didn't say anything to disturb it. We both watched it for what felt like an hour, but I know it was shorter. When it finally flew away, I felt weird. I felt super sad, but also I also felt stupid. Here I was, hoping that my brother was hanging out with me in the form of a freaking bug. *Everything* has his death attached to it now. I'm out here alone with my girlfriend, which should be, like, the best thing *ever*, and I'm trying not to cry, because a freaking butterfly sat on my arm.

Tasha could see that I was getting upset, and she didn't say anything, but she scooted over closer, and rubbed my back softly with her fingertips. Everywhere she touched me, I could still feel it after her hand had moved on. I bent my knees up, and leaned over to rest my head on my arms, and tried to pull myself together, and waited until I didn't feel like crying any more. Then it felt like the butterfly was in my stomach. I turned my face toward hers and leaned over toward her, and we kissed. A real kiss. Like, a make-out kiss. I had wondered what it would be like, and thought it would be pretty awesome, but it was like… infinitely more amazing than I ever imagined.

As we got up to get on our bikes, I looked over, and the butterfly was sitting on the fence, spreading its wings, then it flew up, and disappeared behind the warehouse.

36

At lunch today, I looked up, and Kevin was walking over to our table. It was weird, because he hadn't sat with us since I came back to school. I quickly told everyone to stash their desserts, and when they looked confused, I said, "Kevin!" Their desserts disappeared like it was a magician's trick. He walked up to me and apologized for not coming over to say something already, but that he was sorry to hear about Trevor. I told him I was sorry too, and he said he and his parents had been talking about it, and praying about it, because they thought Trevor was in hell because he took his own life, and that was sinful. He said he would keep praying for us, because that must be the worst thing ever knowing your brother was in hell.

I was speechless. I just sat there with my mouth open. I was so shocked I couldn't say anything.

Keziah goes, "What is wrong with you, Kevin?! Why would you say something so stupid?! You have no business talking to Cody like that! Not to mention that you are *wrong*! If you are worshiping a god who would punish a kid who was sick, you're worshiping the wrong god!"

Kevin mumbled something about how he was just trying to tell me that he had been praying for me, and wandered away.

Keziah was right, of course, but I felt sick. I felt like I was going to throw up. Tasha asked me if I was okay, but I couldn't talk. I seriously didn't know if I was going to bust out crying or spew. Or both. It was one of the worst things that anyone has said to me, and he said it in the cafeteria while other people were around. Now people from other tables were staring, and Tasha and Keziah were both crying, and Ryan looked like he wanted to punch Kevin in the face.

I hadn't even thought about what he said. I hadn't thought about the fact that there were people who thought that Trev committed a sin and was being punished for all eternity. I mean, even though I knew better, it made me feel awful to think other people were so judgmental and stuff.

I had all these thoughts in my head, and I was freaked out because more and more people were looking, and everything started sounding muffled, like I was under water, and I couldn't breathe. I got up and stumbled, and Tasha caught me, and she, Ryan, and Keziah tried to help me toward the door. I felt strong arms reach under me, as Mr. Blackwell picked me up and carried me down to the nurse's office.

I was lying on her couch when Ms. Edous walked in. She's the art teacher, and I've never had one of her classes, but I knew who she was because Trev had her for classes. She pulled a chair right up next to me, and put her hand on my forehead, and said, "My big brother died from suicide. I know how you feel, Cody. I *know*." She had the nurse turn down the lights, and she held my hand, and breathed with me, and talked about how awful it was. How unfair. How lost and alone she was when it happened to her. How even though she was surrounded by friends and family and people at school, she felt like she wasn't really a part of anything. She felt the stares. The judgment. Heard the whispers. How she tried and tried to ignore them, but she still knew they were there. That it wasn't just about missing someone she loved so much, because that would have been more than enough already, but the constant worry about what everyone else was thinking about him too. About her. About her Mom and Dad.

It was such a relief to find someone who went through the same thing. Her feelings are my feelings too, and knowing that someone else gets it – I mean *really* gets it – it just made me feel better.

I had calmed down by the time Mom got there. Ms. Edous talked to her, and Mom hugged her and thanked her for coming to help me. She apologized for not reaching out sooner, and said she hadn't told anyone at school about it, but that she was ready to help us all any time we needed it. They exchanged numbers, and she promised to come visit so that Mom and Dad could talk to her too.

When we came out of the room, Tasha was waiting there with my backpack. She dropped it, and came over and hugged me. I told her to tell Keziah I said thank you for saying to Kevin what I couldn't say.

On the way home, Mom and I talked about how nice it was to have someone to talk to who really understood what we were going through. I don't think that either of us had really realized until that point, just how alone we felt. Of course, we both feel bad for her too. Mom said nothing can just be simple when it comes to suicide. She said she even felt guilty for being relieved to have someone else share their pain. It's all so complicated.

I had a headache by the time I got home, so I took some Tylenol, and laid down on the couch for a bit. I fell asleep, and woke up when Dad got home. He and Mom sat on either side of me, and we ate Chinese take-out. Then they helped me with my homework just to get it over with.

I feel bad that I scared them again when they are already going through so much, but I don't know what to do about it. I guess it's just one more thing to add to the list of things I already feel guilty about.

I know what Dad meant when he said, "I don't know how to do this." I feel the same way. It's like I keep getting punched in the face over and over again. Like I'm in a boxing match, but I don't have any training, and my opponent is big and brutal.

I watched a fight on TV one time where this dude was just getting pummeled. It was horrible. I don't know how he did it, but he just kept getting knocked down, then he would get back up again, and go in for more. It seemed never-ending watching him getting hit over and over and over again. Sometimes he would get in a decent hit, but it never seemed to do much to help him. By the end, he was just stumbling around, looking like he was about to fall over. I couldn't understand why he didn't just lay down, and let it end.

It makes more sense to me now. I'm living it. I just keep getting up. I keep going. It's all I can do. Mom and Dad need it. My friends need it. I need it.

Sometimes I get knocked down, and have days where I don't want to get back up. Days where it seems pointless. Days where I'm stumbling along in pain. Days where I know I'm going to get pummeled, and no matter how hard I try to fight back, I'm going to lose.

But I can't stay down. I can't lose hope. I can't. I've lost too much already.

My family has lost too much.

So, I get up. I go to school. I do the best I can to pretend that everything is okay.

I've never been so tired in my whole life.

37

Today was a better day at school. It felt like people were looking at me a little more than usual, and I could see them stop talking sometimes when I walked by, but I'd figured it would be like that, so I was more ready for it.

When I was at lunch, I looked over, and Kevin was sitting all by himself. It was like every cafeteria scene in every angsty teen movie where the bully gets his comeuppance.

I love that word. Comeuppance. I got it from Trev. He used to love to say things like "fisticuffs" instead of "fight," or "comeuppance" instead of "gets what's coming to him." This one time, Mom asked him if he had his water bottle for school, and he said, "There is no need, Mother. I shall slake my thirst at the fountain."

Wait, where was I? Oh, that's right. Kevin. People were walking around him like he wasn't there. Just avoiding him like he had the plague. I guess word got around about what he said yesterday, and people are mad. I mean, there's a part of me that's like, "Good! That's what you get for being a douche!" but the other part of me feels kind of bad for him.

Ryan saw me staring at him, and he goes, "No. Don't do it, Cody! I know that look! Don't you dare go over there! Dude, he doesn't deserve you going over to let him off the hook. Plus, I have homemade salted caramel brownies, and I don't want to risk him following you back over here and eating them!"

But it was too late. I had to do it. When I got there, he looked up at me and stopped eating. I watched as a big drop of mustard fell onto his gray t-shirt. *Ugh.* It was impossible not to feel sorry for the guy.

He said, "I'm sorry, Cody. I know what I said was stupid. I just thought if I could say something that made you understand I really did feel bad for you, and that I just hadn't known what to say before, it might help."

I said, "Dude, how did you think that telling me that you thought my brother was in hell for all eternity was going to help me? How could that possibly have made me feel better?"

And he looked up at me and blinked a few times and said, "I just thought you knew. I thought it was something everyone knew. It's just the way it is, you know? I thought that it must be the worst part of what you were going through, you know? If it was me, that would be the worst part, and I wanted you to know that I understood it. I don't know... I wanted to say something more than 'I'm sorry,' you know? It didn't seem like enough to say just that."

It made sense in a weird way. I mean, it made sense in a Kevin kind of way.

But that didn't make it okay.

So, I told him that not everyone believed what he believed. That Keziah was right. The god I believe in wouldn't punish a sick kid. I just don't believe that. I also told him that it didn't matter what he believed anyway. That's just not something you would say to someone who had a loss like that. Just say you're sorry. Just say it sucks. Just say your family is upset about it, and thinking about us, and praying for us. That's

enough. The truth is that there isn't anything anyone can say to

make it better. Nothing. But just knowing that people are

willing to try is nice. Unless they say something colossally

stupid like he did.

He nodded his head, and thanked me for coming over to

talk to him. I started to walk away and he said, "Hey, can I

come sit with you guys?"

I looked over his shoulder at my group.

My people.

The ones who understood me.

The ones who stood up for me.

The ones who had my back.

Their eyes were huge, and they were shaking their

heads to tell me not to bring him with me. Ryan was holding up

the salted caramel brownie, Tasha was pointing at it, and

rubbing her stomach, and Keziah was putting the palms of her

hands together in front of her like she was begging me to just

walk away. Kevin turned to look back at them, and they all

quickly acted like they were deep in conversation.

I nearly lost it. I had to look away from them, and put my head down to act like I was really thinking about it so I wouldn't laugh in his face. When I pulled myself together, I looked back up at him, and said, "No. No, you can't sit with us. I accept your apology, and I will eventually get over it, but right now, I'm still pretty mad. What you said was hurtful, and I don't want to sit with you right now."

He nodded his head and went back to eating. Nothing comes between Kevin and lunch.

I walked back over to sit with them and finish eating. Pretty soon Kevin got up, walked over, and put his hand down on the table right next to me. When I looked down, he had left a Little Debbie Oatmeal Cream Pie.

His favorite.

38

Today I went to the warehouse after school and climbed the fence, which I've been doing when I come here alone. It's getting easier. I always look for the butterfly again, but I haven't seen it since the first time. I don't know what I thought would happen. Like, I'd show up, and it would be here waiting for me every day or something, I guess. Stupid. I didn't really believe in that sort of thing, but in that moment, I wanted to. I wanted to believe it more than anything. I wanted to know that he thought I was doing the right thing by working up the courage to climb to the top. That he was proud of me. That he was... here. Like somehow, a part of him was here with me. I'm jealous of people who have visitation dreams. Of people who say they feel like the person they've lost is always with them.

I don't feel that. I don't feel it at all. All I feel is the opposite. I just feel his absence. I feel an emptiness where he used to be. As I sat there, trying to decide if I was going to try the climb today, I was feeding Kevin bits of his dry food on my knee again, and he did the little head butt, then he rubbed the side of his face on my leg. He backed up and looked at me, then came over and rubbed the other side of his face, and I could hear him purr. I didn't want to ruin the moment, so I just sat still and realized I was holding my breath. When I let it out, it startled him, and he backed away.

I walked over to the building and studied the pipework. Where the pipes were connected to each other, there were pieces that they added to hold them together, and the pieces of metal were bigger around than the pipe, so it made like a little ridge there that I could put my feet on. I reached up with both hands, and held on, while I put one foot on either side of the connector, and was able to stand up, holding on to the pipe. I reached up to the next connector with my hands, wrapped my legs around the pipe, and shimmied up until my feet were at the next connector that I could rest my feet on. I worked my way up to the awning above the door. It was a couple of feet over from the pipe, which seemed like a mile away. I reached one hand out to grab the metal bar on the frame of the awning, and tried to swing over to it, but my hands were slippery from nervous sweat, and I lost my grip and fell to the ground. I was only a few feet up, so it didn't hurt, but it frustrated me.

Mom and Dad would be freaking out right now if they knew I was even thinking about doing this. It's not that I'm worried about getting grounded or whatever, I just know that they would be really scared and upset about it. I get that, but... I just feel like this is something that I need to do for Trev. I also need to do it for me. It just feels right. Terrifying... but right.

Next time, I'm going to try to toss my backpack up on the awning so it's not weighing me down. Then when I get to the awning – and I *will* get there – I'll toss it on up to the first balcony.

It feels good to have a plan.

I'm coming, Trev.

I promise.

39

When I was leaving for school this morning, Mom told me that Jackie was coming over. I was like, "Who's Jackie?" She was talking about Ms. Edous. She and Mom have been talking on the phone and messaging and stuff. Mom has been seeing a therapist, and she likes him, but she said that talking to Ms. Edous is helping her more than therapy because she's been through the same loss. It makes sense. I know she helped me feel better when I was in the nurse's office.

Mom said to just meet her in the art room after school, and I could ride home with her. It's cool, I guess, but kind of weird too. I mean, I don't really know her, but I feel like I do since we both lost our brothers the same way.

When I got to her room, she was talking to some students at her desk, so I just wandered around looking at the stuff that was on the walls and shelves. She had student drawings, paintings, and sculptures everywhere. I was looking at some ceramics stuff when I saw Trev's name on a little card next to a sculpture of a cat. It was orange with dark orange stripes, and its mouth was open wide with teeth hanging down. It looked like a bird house, which made me smile. It's definitely something he would have done. It was really good for someone in middle school, and it was funny to see how much his art changed as he went through high school. It was cool to see one of his pieces that I'd never seen before. I couldn't stop staring at it. I reached out to touch it, but stopped myself in case I wasn't supposed to. I guess she saw me, and she said, "It's okay, Cody. You can touch it. Pick it up if you want to." She sent the other students away, walked over, and put it on a desk near me. I put both of my hands on it, and pictured him working on it. When he was creating something, his forehead would wrinkle up, and his mouth would turn down a little bit. He looked like he was frowning, like he was mad, but I knew he was just concentrating. When he tried to look at whatever he was working on from different angles, he looked like a dog when you make a weird noise, and it tilts its head from side to side. I told him that one time, and he went, "*Aaroo*?!" just like Scooby Doo. It made me smile to remember that. Then my eyes were stinging.

Ms. Edous asked me if I wanted to take it home with me, but I said no. I liked knowing it was there. That's where he wanted it to be. I liked that more people would be seeing it there than they would at our house. I told her that, and she nodded, and said, "It's important for him to be remembered, isn't it?" I could only nod my head.

On the way home, she asked me if I'd had any more anxiety attacks, and I said no. She said she had them when her brother died too. She told me that he had hung himself in their garage at home, and that even though she wasn't the one who had found him, she still couldn't help but picture it. That it felt like she had seen it. And even now sometimes the image sneaks up on her, like when she's trying to go to sleep at night, she sees it. I told her I did the same thing. I wasn't there, but I can't help but see it in my head too.

I asked her if she ever got mad.

She goes, "You're kidding, right? Sometimes I'm furious. Then I feel guilty. Then I'm furious again, because I feel guilty again."

I was like, "Get out of my brain," and she laughed.

Her brother, John didn't leave a note either. He just did it. I mean, they knew he was struggling and stuff, but they didn't really get any answers as to why it happened that day. She said they never really got any closure. I had heard that word, and I knew it meant to like, close something, like when a store goes out of business or whatever, but I didn't really understand how that applied to grieving for someone. Like, I don't get how closure works emotionally, I guess. Do we reach a point where we just... move on? Like, "okay. I'm done. I'm ready to put this behind me."

She sighed and said, "I hate that word. It implies that you're over it. That you are ready to close that door and that's that. I don't think it works that way when you lose someone that's such an important part of your life. In fact, I don't think I want it to work that way. I don't want to close the door on his life, and just walk away like it didn't happen. I want to remember him. I want to remember the awesome things about my brother. The things that make me smile or laugh. The problem is, when they leave you the way our brothers left us, you can't remember the good parts without also remembering the bad. And the bad... well, it's as bad as it can get. We humans are hardy creatures. It takes a lot to kill us. So, when someone chooses to die, the result can be pretty horrific. Violent even. So, to remember all of the good stuff, but then be unable to get the image of their death out of your head... well, it gets all mixed up together, and you find yourself smiling at a memory, and enjoying the thought of him, then the next thing you know, you're crying because you won't get to make any more memories with him because he decided he needed to leave you behind, and he did it in such an ugly way and left you to deal with the aftermath. He left you on your own to try to figure out how to help your parents. And there's no way to do that. It's impossible. He left you questioning your part in it, even though it had nothing to do with you. Look, I know it wasn't my fault that my brother died. I *know* that. But it still feels like there was something I could have done. Something I missed. The truth of the matter is that I feel like I simply wasn't enough to keep him alive. I know it doesn't make sense. It doesn't have to. It just is."

I told her that I felt the same way about everything she said, and that I was relieved because I had been feeling weird. She laughed, and said, "Oh, don't get me wrong. It's plenty weird. All of it. It's all just *weird*. But now you know that you're not alone in your weirdness. I'm weird too."

It helped. I mean, it was nice to find another person who understood my world of weirdness right now. Of course, It made it a little weirder that she was a teacher at my school. I told her that, and she laughed and said, "It is, isn't it? How do you think I feel pouring out my soul to a seventh grader?" It turns out that no one else at school except Mr. Blackwell knew her story, and she only told him after talking to me in the nurse's office. When I asked her why she told me, she said, "You needed me to tell you, and I needed to tell it. I get tired of feeling alone too. I still struggle with it all the time."

For some reason, I was surprised by that. I asked her how long ago her brother died, and she said fifteen years. He's been gone longer than I've been alive, and she still struggles

with it. To think about how I probably won't ever get over

Trev's death is sort of, I don't know… It's hard to picture it.

But to hear another person, an adult, talk about how it's still

hard… it just, it makes it seem more real. The never-ending-

ness of it. The fact that I'll be old, like, thirty something, with

my own family and a job and stuff, and it will still be a big part

of my life feels… I don't know. I guess it makes me feel sad

and discouraged and also a little bit mad.

Oh, and hey! There's the guilt too. Always. Always the

guilt.

40

I got to go to Tasha's house today after school. Mrs. Corte put us together on a project, and she gave us class time to work on it, so we were basically done with it when class was over, which was awesome, because we just got to hang out and play video games and stuff until dinner time. We played old games on the Nintendo Wii, like Fruit Ninja. It was so much fun. Her dad came in to try it, and every time he would slash at the fruit, he would yell, "*Hi-ya!*" He was trying really hard to embarrass her, but I just thought it was hilarious. Both her parents and her sister were home, and they were all really nice.

Tasha was showing me her room, and I looked over and saw she had a recorder on her dresser. You know, one of those plastic flute things that everyone gets in elementary school, and you learn to play *Hot Cross Buns* on it. She said it was her sister's hand-me-down. I laughed, and told her that I got a lot of my brother's hand-me-downs, but I got my own recorder because Trev played his with his left nostril. I showed her a video on my phone of him playing the beginning part of the song, *My Heart Will Go On*, from the Titanic movie. We were all at the dinner table, and you could hear us all laughing while my mom recorded it. When Tasha stopped laughing, she said, "He's really good!" I agreed and told her how he said he took the difficulty up a notch by playing it with his left nostril instead of his right... because he was right-handed, so he was probably "right nostrilled" too.

She told me that she wished she could have met him. I wish she could have too.

When her dad dropped me off and I walked into the house, the first thing I noticed was how quiet it was. Mom and Dad were home, but they weren't talking. There was no music. No TV. Just... quiet. I realized that the quiet emptiness in the house is just the way it is now. Tasha's house is busy and full of life, and ours is, I don't know, full of... death, I guess. Mom and Dad tried to make conversation and asked how school was, and if I'd had a good time, but it felt like they were just asking because that's what was expected of them. After a few minutes, Mom wandered upstairs to her bedroom, and Dad went into the computer room.

I miss my brother, but I also miss just *living*. I miss the noise that we used to have in the house. I miss Mom playing old 80s music while she cooked dinner, and hearing her sing along. I miss Dad coming home, and kicking off his shoes at the door, and giving a big sigh because he was relieved to be home. Now it seems like he's relieved to be at work. I miss having real conversations about real things. It feels like we all just talk about stuff that doesn't matter, because it's too hard to talk about the stuff that does.

I guess this is what they call the "New Normal."

It freaking sucks.

41

The phone rang during dinner today, and Mom answered it, then took it in the other room to talk. When she came back in, she told me that it was Kevin's mom. She called to apologize for what Kevin said in the cafeteria. Dad said that he has had people make a few comments that have been really dumb, too. Like, this one lady at work said that her brother had been really depressed, and died from suicide, and she was relieved that he was no longer in pain, and one day he would feel the same way about Trev's death. Dad said he would never be relieved that his son wasn't with us anymore. Then Mom said that a lady who heard about it that she barely knew asked her if she was going to try to have another baby. Dad and I were both shocked by that one. We said, "*Whaaaat?!?!*" at exactly the same time in the same way, and we couldn't help but laugh. I mean, seriously! We didn't lose a pet. It's not like getting another puppy. You can't replace a human being, you know? I asked her what she said, and she said she just looked her in the eye, and said, "Ummm... no," and we laughed again.

We talked about some of the awkward moments that we've had, like at his memorial where everyone wants to say something and hug you and you're just trying to get through it. I told them about this one lady who mom had been friends with who hugged me for *waaaaayyyy* too long. Like, I started the hug with my arms around her too, then I sort of patted her back to try to let her know that hugging time was over, but she just stood there, squeezing me, and sort of rocking back and forth a little. I remember looking around desperately for someone to save me, but I was on my own. Trapped in her awkwardly long embrace with my arms dangling at my sides.

As I told the story, Mom got to laughing so hard she was wheezing, and when she could talk, she said, "She did the same thing to me!"

Then we talked about how to break out of the awkward hug. I said you could do it like a self-defense move, where you bring your arms up, crossed in front of you, and then break them open. I demonstrated my maneuver with Dad hugging me. Then Mom said you could do the Toddler Maneuver, like when you try to pick up a toddler who doesn't want to be picked up, and they just go limp, and slide out of your arms. She had Dad get back up, and they moved to the carpet. He put his arms around her, and she just went all limp, and slid to the floor.

Seeing my mom act like that again, and my dad laughing so hard he was doubled over with his hands on his knees was just the best. When we all calmed down, Dad took Mom's hand, and helped her up, then he just hugged her tight, and kissed her forehead.

At that moment, I felt like maybe we would be okay someday. Like maybe someday the moments like this would happen more often than the other moments. I know it's going to be a long time before that happens, but at least I had a little bit of hope, you know? I mean, like, I can't expect to wake up one morning and be over it, because I don't think that will ever happen. I won't ever be over it. So, I guess the best I can do right now is just, like, accept and I guess... *appreciate* the days where I feel a little better than I did yesterday. I have to let myself appreciate those days, and be okay with that.

We learned a little bit about Buddhism in history class. We were talking about religions, and Mr. Karinen talked about how even though he's not a Buddhist, there are some parts of it that he really likes, and that he uses. Like, he has what's called a mantra. That means he has a sentence he says to himself every morning before he comes to work. He says, "Today, I will choose kindness." I think it must help him, because there are some real jerks in my class, and Mr. Karinen is always super nice to them, and the weird thing is, a couple of weeks into class, they actually changed. They were nicer to him, and treated him better than they treated some of the other teachers.

Anyway, I think that I'm going to try it. A mantra. Maybe I can say, "Today I will be happy."

Nah. Because I know I'll have days where I won't be. I need to have the sad days too, and know that that's okay too.

"Today, I will accept my feelings."

I'll be okay with it if I'm upset or mad, and I'll also be okay with it if I am having a good day, and I will try not to feel guilty about it.

"Today, I will accept my feelings."

That's it.

42

Today was Dad's birthday. We rode our bikes to the warehouse to feed the cats and have a picnic there. I know it sounds weird, but Dad said that's what he wanted to do. He's been spending more time at home, and we've all been talking a little bit more about Trev. We gave the cats their food, and then we sat on a blanket to eat and Kevin just sat there, looking confused for a minute on the other side of the fence.

Mom said, "That's weird. Isn't he the one who usually comes running over first?"

I didn't want to tell her that he had gotten used to me climbing the fence, so he was waiting for me there, because then I'd have to tell her everything.

I just said, "Yeah… that's him. He's weird." I'm a terrible liar. He eventually came over and ate with the others, but he still went back through the hole to the other side, and stared at me like, "Come on, dude!"

It's always been hard buying gifts for Dad because not only does he usually just go out and get whatever he needs, but it was especially hard this time because it's the first celebration we've had since Trev died, and I don't think any of us knew quite what to do. I ended up getting him a bike helmet cover that looked like a Viking helmet. He laughed when he opened it. I was going to get him a shirt that said, "Don't startle me, I fart easily," but I figured he'd like the helmet cover better. Mom got him tickets to go see an old music group called REO Speedwagon. I didn't know who they were, but Mom said that they were the first concert that they went to when they were dating. I told them I was shocked that they were still a band and still having concerts, because I figured they'd be in a nursing home by now. I probably shouldn't have said that out loud, but I didn't think that until after it was already out of my mouth.

Mom said, "Thanks a lot!"

And Dad just said, "*Ouch!!*"

They both laughed though, then Mom put her lips over her teeth, so she'd look like she was toothless, and she hunched over and started singing, "I can't fight this feelin' any loooonger…" like an old woman, and Dad did the same thing with his mouth, but he kept yelling, "What?! Huh?! What did she say?" It was hilarious. That's the Mom and Dad I'm used to. I've missed them.

We didn't buy birthday cards, because we just couldn't find the right ones. Trev always got the best cards, because they were always for the wrong thing. Like one Mother's Day, he bought a card for Mom that said, "Happy Birthday, Grandma!" Dad got one last year that said, "Mazel Tov!" on the front, and it was for a girl's Bat Mitzvah. The last card I got from him said, "Happy Retirement!" The best. We all looked forward to seeing what he was going to come up with.

Dad didn't mention not getting a card, but I know he knew why.

Before we got on our bikes to ride home, Dad reached in his pocket, and pulled out a little Lego guy. He walked over, and dug a little hole right up against the fence, and put the guy in it, then covered it up. He said he wanted to leave something there, but flowers just didn't seem like the thing to leave. Trev loved Legos. They were his favorite thing when he was little. It was the perfect thing. We were all crying, and standing there looking down at the tiny grave, and Dad said, "I miss you, son. I wish you were here to congratulate me on my Bat Mitzvah."

43

Me, Tasha, Ryan, and Keziah all have a group text.

We've been talking about how cool it would be to go to this

old arcade called The Fun Factory, and then hang out at Ryan's

after. We finally got all of our parents to say it was okay, and

we did it.

It was the best night of my life. For reals. We played a

bunch of old video games, like Pong, Joust, Pac Man and

Donkey Kong. Then we had an air hockey tournament, which I

won. Keziah and Tasha played Dance Dance Revolution, and

Keziah was somehow able to play amazingly well, and talk

smack to Tasha at the same time. Tasha was laughing too hard

to play seriously. We all played Skeeball, then we took all of

our change and played the game where you put in a quarter,

and it falls down with the other quarters, then this metal rake thing pushes them off the edge. We got a ton of tickets, and turned them in for some inflatable hammers, and a big Surprise Box.

When we got home and finished hitting each other with the hammers, we opened the box. It had a pair of pink baby socks, a bracelet that said "Katherine" on it, some "Just My Size Pantyhose," party invitations with a picture of one of those triangle glasses with a stem and an olive in it. I think it's called a martini glass. There was a tiny bottle of water in a box with a picture of the Virgin Mary on it labeled "Holy Water," and some hair scrunchie things. The best thing though, was the Dr. Laura talking doll. None of us knew who Dr, Laura was, but when you push the button, she says things like, "Don't bring home an elephant, and then complain because it won't sit on your lap and purr." "Don't argue with me! It makes me testy." And "Now, go do the right thing!" By the time the box was empty, we were all laughing so hard we were crying.

Kyle must have heard us as he was walking by the game room, and he stopped and said, "Whoa... girls! I can't believe you two losers got girlfriends! You're an inspiration to losers everywhere!" Then he walked over, grabbed a slice of pizza, and smacked Ryan on the back of the head. Then as he left the room, he mumbled something about not getting anyone knocked up. At least that's what I think he said. He was saying it with his mouth crammed full of pizza. It was nice to see that he was back to his old self. "Nice Kyle" weirded me out more than a little bit.

We spent the rest of the evening watching one of the Avengers movies. I couldn't even tell you which one. Ryan and Keziah were on a beanbag chair on the floor, and me and Tasha were on the couch. We pretty much made out through the whole movie.

I didn't want the night to end.

But now I'm home, and Mom and Dad have gone to bed, and I'm recording in Trev's room because if he was here, I'd be telling him everything that happened. I guess this is my way of doing that. I'm trying to let it be okay to have had fun tonight. It's hard to push down the guilt, but I'm working on it. It's the best I can do right now.

I had a really good day. I know how much Trev loved the old arcade. We always laughed at how they used to have that giant meat slicer like the ones in the grocery store deli for like, 4000 tickets or something like that. It's gone. Someone must have saved up for it. He would have found that hilarious. In fact, I almost pulled out my phone to text him about it.

I miss him so much. Even though I was having fun with my friends, I thought about him.

I always do.

44

I woke up this morning feeling like today was the day. This is it. Today I'm going to finish the climb. I pulled out the chalk bag that I had Trev's ashes in, and I put a little in a different baggie. I grabbed some cat food, put it all in my backpack, and told Mom and Dad I was going to feed the cats, then I left.

I was so used to climbing the fence that I was over it in no time, and I sat and fed the cats. Kevin has gotten so much more comfortable that he rubbed up against my hand today. I reached out to pet him after that, and he backed away, then he came back over and let me scratch his head for a bit. I think it calmed both of us down.

I finally walked over and tossed my backpack up onto the awning. Now I was totally committed. I at least had to get up there to get my backpack. I took one last look around to make sure no one was there, then I climbed the pipework just like I did the other day. When I got to the point where I could reach over and push off to grab the metal frame of the awning, I took a big breath and just went for it.

I missed.

But this time, I got my fingers on the frame, I just didn't get a good enough grip to hold myself up. I should have put some chalk on my hands so they would grip better, but of course the chalk was in my backpack on the awning. I climbed up again, but this time, I went a little bit higher on the pipework and when I pushed off, I was sort of going down toward the awning, so it wasn't as much of a jump, and I did it. I was hanging off of the frame. I pulled my legs up, and got one leg over, then scooched myself over where I was against the building, and I could sort of push off of it to pull myself up to reach one hand on the top of the awning. I got both hands up on it, and started pulling myself sort of across it, until I could get my knee up there.

I did it. I was standing on top of it, looking up at the balcony above me. I could reach it. All I had to do was pull myself up to it, and then the balconies were all connected by stairs. It would be just like doing a pull up.

I suck at doing pull ups.

And I was terrified. I kept facing the wall, so I wouldn't have to look down. I was just standing there, panting, and thinking, "Come on, dude... If you're going to give me a sign, now would be the time."

I turned around.

Nothing happened. No butterfly. No sunlight breaking through the clouds to shine down on me. No voice in my head telling me to go ahead and do it. Just me standing there breathing like I needed an asthma inhaler.

I grabbed the chalk out of the bag and put some on my palms, then I closed it up, put it in my backpack, and tossed it up on the balcony.

I reached up and put my hands on the floor of the balcony above me, and started pulling myself up. My arms were shaking, and I was grunting, but I was able to get to the point where I could put one elbow up, then the other one. I had to just hang there for a bit and rest before I could swing my leg up there. Once I was able to do that, I got my other leg up, and I made it.

I just laid there on my back and shook. I was in a restaurant one time, and the server asked this old guy if he wanted more coffee, and he said, "If I have one more cup of coffee, I'll be shaking like a dog crappin' a peach pit!" I know that's super gross, but if you've ever seen a dog struggling to go to the bathroom. you know exactly what he was talking about. That's how I felt right now. Every part of me was shaking. I was vibrating inside and out.

I was worried that I might be working myself up for a panic attack, but I was able to start to control my breathing, and in a few minutes, I was feeling a little better. I was still nervous, but I felt like the hardest part was over, and I was right. From here, I could climb the stairs, then pop through a hole onto the next balcony up. I put on my backpack, and climbed the rest of the stairs with no problem. I came out at the top, and I just stood there for a bit and looked around.

The roof was dirty and stuff, and you could tell that no one ever came up there. There weren't even leaves on it, because it was higher than the trees, I guess. I put my backpack down, and started looking around to see if I could find a note or anything that he might have left. I walked around the whole roof. I looked everwhere.

There was nothing there.

Nothing.

No note.

No answer as to why he did it.

No goodbye.

Nothing.

I guess I shouldn't have expected anything, but... I kind of did. At least I hoped I would find something up here that would make it make more sense.

I started to walk over to the edge, and just the thought of it made me feel dizzy. It made my stomach sink. I wanted to stand in the last place he stood. I wanted to see the last thing he saw, but where he felt drawn to the edge, I was terrified of it.

How? How could he do it? I just don't understand.

Maybe if I did understand it, it would only be because I felt the same way. I don't. I don't feel that way. I don't ever want to feel that way. I just know that he must have been desperate. Desperate and determined. He needed to make his pain stop. He had to have had no choice, because why else would he do this? It must have been absolutely unbearable.

I had to turn away.

So, there I sat. In the middle of the roof, crying. Talking out loud to my brother. Asking why, and getting no answer. Just the wind and the dirty roof and the sky above me.

I had really hoped that climbing up there would change things for me. I mean, I wanted to sprinkle his ashes, and leave a piece of him there, but... I don't know... I also wanted more than that.

I wanted to feel closer to him.

I wanted answers. I wanted to know why. Why that day? Why did he lose hope? Why couldn't he stay? Why couldn't he see that he wouldn't always feel that way? Why did he have to leave all of us feeling so empty?

I guess maybe my answer is that there is no answer. Maybe he couldn't even explain it.

That doesn't seem like enough, but I suppose it's going to have to be, because it's all I've got.

I pulled myself together and stood up. I took baby steps until I was a couple of feet away from the drop off, and I closed my eyes and breathed deep for a few seconds. I took the last couple of steps, and looked out over the edge. I felt like I was swaying - like it was pulling at me. My stomach did a flip, and I sat down, and scooted backwards a few feet.

It wasn't quite as scary being down low, so I got down on my hands and knees, and crawled back over. I pulled his ashes out of my pocket, and laid down flat on my belly. I pushed forward until my elbows were at the edge. I opened the baggie, turned it upside down, and let the wind carry my brother away.

As I looked out to watch his ashes fall, a butterfly floated by. I suddenly felt Trevor there with me. Finally. Part of me felt relieved, and part of me felt like I was being an idiot, but my mantra is to accept my feelings, no matter what they are. I could feel him, so I'm accepting that. I may not have gotten the answers I wanted, but I did feel closer to him, and that's one of the reasons I did the climb.

I know exactly what he would say if he was really here. At the gym, he always made me stay until I climbed to the top of the wall, even when I was ready to go home. He would be belaying me on the ropes below, and as I climbed, he would yell, "I know it's hard, dude, but I got you. I won't let you fall! It's a mind thing- not a muscle thing. You can do it! Your brain is trying to stop you, but you gotta push past it. You're gonna make it."

When I would get back on the ground, he would hold up his fist for a bump, and I would do the same, and we would slow motion miss bumping fists, and pretend to punch each other in the face. I would say, "Dude, that was so hard!" And he would say, "Yeah. I know it is, but you did it. I'm proud of you, Cody. You ready to go?"

"Yeah. I'm ready. It's time to go home."

END

A note from the author

On Thursday, January 25, 2018, my 18-year-old son, Trevor, who was an avid rock climber, scaled a warehouse in the Port of Los Angeles, and jumped to his death. My husband, Brad, my surviving son, Cody, and I have been left to try to make sense of his suicide. We are dealing with the loss, and trying to move forward, each in our own unique way.

I was doing some research online, and trying to find help for Cody, when I realized that there really isn't a lot out there for people who have lost a sibling to suicide. I thought to myself, "Well... you can complain and do nothing, or you can choose to do something about it."

This book is what I chose to do.

I have never considered myself a writer, but I had been sharing stories about Trevor with my friends and family on Facebook, and I came to realize how very important it was to let people know who he was. I hate the idea of my brilliant, hilarious son being remembered for his final act, when his life was so much more than that. I also realized that sharing my experience with his death, and connecting to other people who suffered the same tragedy made me feel less alone. So many others have experienced loss to suicide, and the unique feelings that come with that loss. Those connections... those "OMG, me too!" moments, have kept me moving forward without leaving his memory behind.

Writing this book has been a gift to me. Even though it is a work of fiction, there is a great deal of Trevor in it. It's not his story completely, but his personality is there. His humor is there, as is his illness. This is a way for me to share a little bit about my son, and honor his memory. The writing process has also been very therapeutic for me, and if it helps one survivor feel less alone, I will be fulfilled.

The thought of sharing this book with the world is quite honestly frightening for me. I have chosen to share this process with a very small group of people, and I want to thank them for their help and support. Thank you to my friend, Sonnjea Blackwell, for helping me edit and format my work. She's been there since this was just an idea in my head, and her technical help has been great, but her friendship has been invaluable. Thank you to Ken Lay who helped me with the last round of editing. Your insight and honesty have been such a tremendous help in this process. I had a couple of "I don't like that idea, but I'll try it just to see... Well, crap. He was right." moments that really improved the story. To Paul Knox... BEH! I have made most of the changes they suggested, but I kept a few things the way they were. If you find errors, blame me. They're most likely my fault. I also want to thank my talented brother-in-law, Steven Bassett, for reading my book, for being my cheerleader, my friend, and for the cover design. It's exactly what I hoped it would be. I also want to give a special thank you to Jackie Edous. I have heard from her every single day since I lost my boy over two years ago, and I can't even begin to express how much that means to me. She's the best.

I could go on and on listing the people who have helped me personally along the way, but I'm so blessed with support that it would take forever, so I'm going to focus on the two that are most near and dear to my heart. Thank you to Brad and Cody. For everything. I love you both more than I can put into words, and I don't know how I could have gotten through this without you.

Finally… if you are reading this book because you have suffered the loss of a loved one to suicide, I am sorry. Truly. It's devastating. Just like in the book, where each character grieves in his or her own way, you will do the same, and that's ok. There is no right or wrong way to grieve, and there is no timeline. Your grief will be like your fingerprint - uniquely you. It doesn't have to look like anyone else's journey. Take your time, and learn to accept your feelings. It's ok to cry, it's ok to laugh, and it's also ok to not feel much of anything at times too. All of it is normal, and to be expected. You are not alone.

Made in the USA
Middletown, DE
31 July 2020

14087100R00116